patchwork

Tales from Long Lily, 1.5

Tess Carletta

Disclaimer

This novella contains emergency situations including house fires and health crises. It also contains depictions of firefighting work, which have been thoroughly researched. However, inaccuracies are inevitable. The text of this book should not be considered accurate or informative, but has been written with the intention of offering appreciation for small-town first responders, many of whom are volunteers.

Contents

Meet the Simons

From Tallie's scrapbook
(With help from Lewie)

LEWIE SIMON

- 32 years old – the oldest!
- ~~Single Dad~~
- LEGAL GUARDIAN
- Sells houses
- Best friends with Uncle Basie
- Played lacross
- Doesn't like to cook
- Makes good dinners
- I like his hugs

Lewie's truck: "The Centipede"

Maria Simon

- 21 years old
- Goes to Allegheny College
- Learning law and fiber arts
- Has a tattoo Lewie doesn't know about (she doesn't care)
- Volunteers in ~~Amerricor~~ Americorps
- Nice to me :)

Orion Simon

- 18 years old – 12th grade
- They / them / theres
- Has ~~rit rete~~
- RETINITIS PIGMENTOSA
- Canis is there dog
- Likes walking
- Good at finding things
- Has a lot of keys and neckleces

Eliza Simon

- 12 years old – 7th grade
- Making a quilt
- Good at reading stories
- Wants to be a chemist
- Has $3 in overdo library fines
- Favorite food is mac and cheese
- Afraid of bees

Sam

- My twin
- Sam is also 9
- Stinky and smelly
- Collects dead bugs
- Favorite animal is a poisen frog

Tallie Simon

- Me!!! ☺
- I am 9 – 3 grade
- I like to write books
- I am older then Sam
- I want to be an animal vet when I grow up

Meyer Simon

- 7 years old
- Kinda sassy
- ~~Thinks he's smarter then me~~
- Smart
- Wants to take over the family bisness
- Makes good PB and Js

Ethan Simon

- 4 years old
- Pracktically a baby still
- Uncle Kit's favorite (even if he won't say so)
- Still can't write his letters
- Looooves chocolate
- Good at Legos

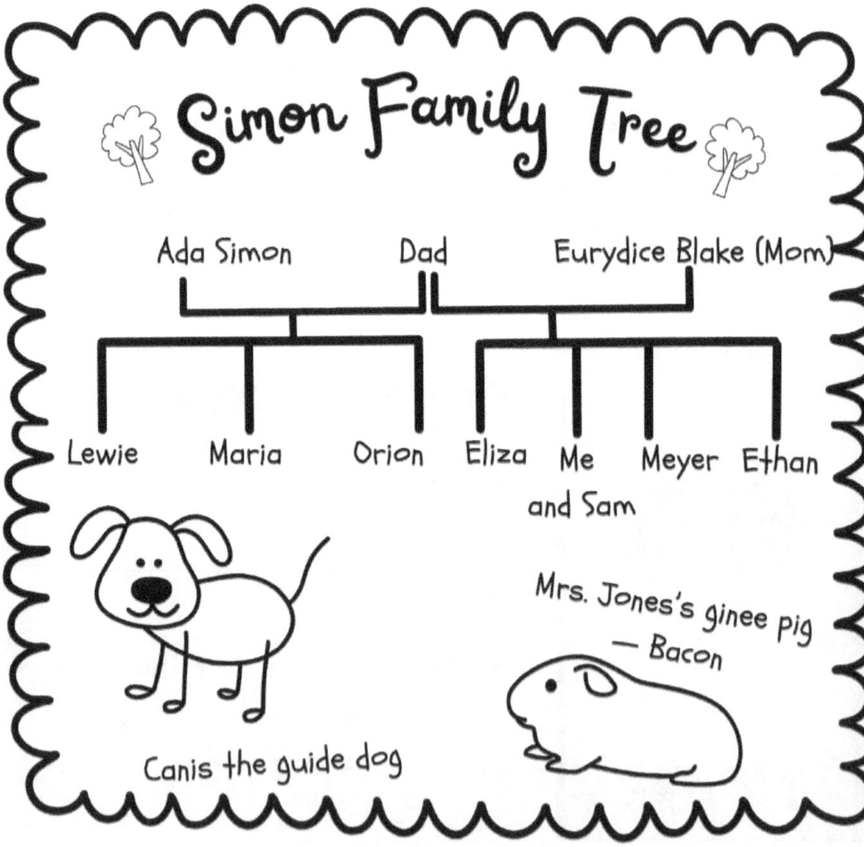

Simon Family Tree

Ada Simon — Dad — Eurydice Blake (Mom)

Lewie • Maria • Orion • Eliza • Me and Sam • Meyer • Ethan

Canis the guide dog

Mrs. Jones's ginee pig — Bacon

patchwork

June, 2025

K IT ELLIOT LOVED HIS HUSBAND.

"These Oreo balls are going to take your pretentious little apple pie and smear it all over the road like mangled roadkill. You're maggot food, Baltimore."

Addendum: Kit loved his husband, even when he was being an overly competitive jackass.

It was big talk from a guy who'd forgotten he was supposed to bring a dessert to Orion Simon's birthday dinner in the first place. Kit had anticipated Basie's slip-up like a prophetic vision and had thrown an extra pie into the oven at Mallory's as a backup. Offended at being so well-known, Basie had insisted on bringing a *second* dessert, swearing left and right that Orion would like his creation better.

Kit didn't think Basie could swing it. With dinner less than two hours away, Basie's options for potential sweets were slim. Paired with Orion's penchant for always acting like they disliked *everything*, Basie was decidedly outta luck.

Or at least, Kit thought so until Basie proved him wrong by throwing his Oreo balls together in thirty minutes flat. After tasting one, Kit discovered the godly combination of crushed Oreos, cream cheese, and melted chocolate proved to be a formidable contender that he hadn't anticipated. In truth, he didn't consider

Oreo balls as a possibility because he hadn't made anything so simple in…possibly ever.

The Oreo balls were only a symptom of a larger problem Kit could not put his finger on—not the confections themselves, but the need for them. Of the Elliot-Yeats duo, Kit *was* the one who never let things fall through the cracks, but that didn't make Basie forgetful, by any means. And yet, in the last three weeks, Basie had overlooked all of the May bills, left a quart of ice cream sitting on the counter overnight, let the irises out front go unwatered, and clean forgot their anniversary. Basie was still apologizing for that last one.

Kit could tell something was on Basie's mind, something he wasn't telling his husband.

He had kind of thought they'd left the whole secret-keeping thing at the marriage altar. It was a nice change of pace after those anxious months of mutually hiding their own secret immortalities, but maybe Basie had stashed a little secret-keeping in his back pocket, after all. The urge to let a gentle question slip between them was dangerously tempting. A simple, *What's bothering you, Basie?* Or, even its safer alternative, *Why don't you tell me what's on your mind?* For foolproof results, *You seem stressed. Why don't you let me rub your back and we can talk about it?* When it came to manipulating Basie for the sake of his own wellbeing, Kit was shameless and adept.

He just had to get the timing right. A family birthday party was decidedly *not* the right time.

That left them where they were now, right in front of the Simon house, Basie tossing around threats of victory and roadkill.

"I am perfectly content with Orion liking your *balls* better than mine," Kit said evenly.

Basie shot him a look. "You're not earning bonus points for off-color jokes."

"I'm not earning points at all, sweetheart. It's not a competition," Kit said calmly, balancing his pie in one hand and Orion's present in the other. This was playing dirty. Basie always listened a little closer when Kit spoke to him with anything resembling affection. "A competition has prizes, rules, and, when baked goods are involved, Mary Berry."

"Don't bring that sweet old lady into this. This is about baking and blood," Basie replied fiercely, marching up the green Victorian's porch steps, abandoning Kit several paces behind.

Kit cleared his throat.

"*And* it's about celebrating a grumpy eighteen-year-old on the day of their birth," Basie relented.

The corner of Kit's mouth quirked. Maybe it wouldn't hurt to play along—just a bit.

"In the event the aforementioned grumpy teenager does select a winner, what spoils will the victor take home?"

Basie halted in front of the old Simon door. He threw a glance over his shoulder, letting his eyes sweep over the full length of Kit's body.

"Well, handsome, I'm sure I'll figure something out."

Kit cocked a brow, heat creeping up his chest. Before he could reach for Basie to give him some ideas, Basie let himself into the house with a shout of, "Where's the birthday bastard?" Kit followed behind, ducking below the low rise door frame.

It had taken until Basie's return from West Virginia for Kit to learn the names of all the Simon children. When they stood side-by-side, it was easy to track the resemblance between all eight siblings. Each of them had the same brown hair, dark enough to get lost against the starless sky. Their skin was warm and pale, smiles full and dimpled.

But it was their bright eyes that gave you a look into the real family similarity: the Simon Knowing, something Kit had been minding his business about.

Because of these similarities between all the children, Kit had an embarrassing habit of getting their names mixed up. When he came to visit, he ran attendance in his head to prevent his century-old brain from any slips.

There was Maria, the emotional and age-sequential buffer between Basie's best friend Lewie and his younger sibling, Orion. She was away at college studying law and, as a fun little twist, fiber arts, which she had decided on a whim. Kit had only seen Maria in pictures, because she chose to spend her summers lending her talent to the AmeriCorps. She'd called Basie's cell once to ask for donations, but that was the only time Kit had ever spoken to her. Her absence meant that when Lewie needed an extra pair of hands for their many extra children, it was Orion who often stepped up to the plate.

Orion was someone Kit went soft at the thought of, only because he knew how to recognize a person who was hurting badly enough, they'd stopped doing anything about it. Kit kept this pity under wraps, knowing it made Orion's skin crawl. They got enough of it after their retinitis pigmentosa diagnosis, and then even more when the scope of their vision disappeared completely, leaving them with blurs of light and smudges. Yet, Kit did not get the sense that it was Orion's blindness that had soured their disposition. Unsure of the true culprit, Kit tried to focus on the things that distracted Orion from their bitterness instead, like their guide dog, Canis, and talking about Pennsylvanian cryptids.

Lewie, Maria, and Orion made up the trifecta of siblings who'd been the original Simon children, the planned offshoots of Luke Simon and his first wife, Ada. The only time Kit had heard anything about Ada was when Lewie had gotten drunk and said, *"Kit, I trust you with my best friend because you love him the way my father loved my mother."* Kit *had* heard about what happened to Luke after Ada's death, how he went mad with grief and went looking for affection in all the wrong places.

That was how the rest of the Simon children came to be: by accident. The rumors were uncomplicated. Luke had been seen loitering around a married Eurydice Blake, smiling at her and complimenting her golden spun hair. Then, before anyone in the town had blinked an eye, Eurydice divorced her husband, married Luke, and carried his baby around in her beautifully swollen belly for less than nine months. Only, when folks told the story, sometimes the order of events got switched around, taking on an unscrupulous tone. Even more hushed was the rumor that Eurydice had always been sweet on Luke—that she'd been *thrilled* when Ada got sick. And Ada knew it.

Now all three of them were gone, a troubled man and the women he loved stuck sharing him.

Kit got the sense that there was an invisible boundary between the Simon Siblings Proper and the Simon Siblings Subsequent. Even if some of them were too young to know *why* the line was there, they kept to their own—Ada versus Eurydice, even beyond the grave. Basie said that was why Lewie worked so hard to keep the family together. They already had enough forces working against them.

The scandal child was Eliza, twelve years old and next-oldest after Orion. The twins came next, Tallie and Sam, who would tell you that they were nine (which they were) and that they were identical (which they were not). Meyer followed close behind, more sensible and wiser than his seven years. He had opinions about local politics and often tried to voice them at town hall meetings. He'd even tried to nominate himself for local election.

Last was Kit's secret favorite, baby Ethan, who had turned four earlier that summer. Ethan had always been a well-behaved child. According to Lewie, he'd been the least maintenance of all the kids, up until recently, when he'd taken to random weeping fits from which he could not be consoled. But Kit had seen enough children grow old to know that colic wasn't a death sentence—even if it happened four years too late.

At present, Eliza was leading Tallie and Sam to wash up for dinner. She tossed an exasperated smile at Kit as she passed, tugging the twins along by the scruff of their shirts to the bathroom. Kit noticed smears of dirt over their tiny hands and under their fingernails, as if they'd just gotten back from making mud pies in the backyard.

"I didn't know you were a wild beast wrangler, Eliza," Kit called to her.

"Remind me to never work at a zoo," she called back, before letting out a screech. "*Samuel Simon*, get your thumb off of that faucet! You're spraying water everywhere! And clean under your fingernails, would you? It looks like worms are gonna pop out from underneath them. Filthy."

Chuckling to himself, Kit found the mile-long dining room table and placed his pie off to the side next to the empty trivets.

"Excuse me, Uncle Kit," said a voice that was equal parts squeaky and annoyed. Kit peered down and found Meyer holding a stack of plates piled so high they covered his face from his ears down. "You're in my way. Can you move?"

"That didn't sound very polite," Lewie cut in, appearing from the back door with a plate overflowing with steak kebabs and golden potatoes, all grilled with perfect crispy edges. "I thought I asked you to set the table, not hit our guests with your attitude."

"I *said* excuse me," Meyer argued.

Lewie slammed the plates on the counter a little too hard.

"I will not have you speaking to me, or our guests, like—"

Basie swooped in to cut off Lewie's glare.

"Hey, hey! No harm done. Let me help you out, little man," Basie suggested quickly. He tossed Kit a look that said, *Free the bees in that man's bonnet or else we're going to get stung!*

Smooth as butter, Basie plucked the plates from Meyer's wobbly hands and began to lay out each setting. "Mey-man, why don't you have one of those Oreo balls and tell me if you like it better than Uncle Kit's apple pie."

"Basie, do not involve my innocent children in your marital disputes," Lewie demanded from the kitchen. The words themselves said, *Ahaha! I'm making a joke,* but the tone betrayed what was probably the real meaning, which Kit imagined to be something like *I am on the verge of a complete and total meltdown.*

Kit arrived in the kitchen just in time to watch Lewie bump into the kebab plate, sending it teetering and tottering right on the edge of the counter. Sliding with his socks, Kit swooped in to lasso the plate before it could shatter on the floor in a mess of marinade, chopped vegetables, and wooden skewers. Lewie watched the whole thing in horror, only to close his eyes when the kebabs escaped catastrophe.

"If you were having a bad parenting day, you could've called. We would've come sooner," Kit offered, leaning his hip against the cabinet.

"I'm not having a bad parenting day," insisted Lewie.

Right on cue, Ethan, the youngest of the Simon kids, sprinted full speed into the kitchen. Kit had just enough time to process the chocolate all over Ethan's face and his wobbly feet catching on his long pant legs, before Ethan smacked his face right into the back door. Ethan stared at the hardwood in complete betrayal, frowning where the chocolate on his face had smeared onto the door. He turned to Lewie with a blank expression—then began to *wail*.

Whatever Lewie's first reaction was going to be, it was not going to be good, so Kit scooped the preschooler into his arms and said, "Oh, you're alright. Just a wee scare. You're a silly thing, running through the house like a cheetah. Ethan, can you tell me what noise a cheetah makes?"

Through tears and snot, Ethan heaved a watery breath and gave a very pitiful *meow*.

"Not a very ferocious cheetah, but I'll take it." Kit scanned his gaze over all the itsy-bitsy details of Ethan's face, checking for bruises, blood, and a crooked nose. He was not a doctor, but he did think Ethan would live. "You're not bleeding anywhere, though you *are* covered in chocolate. How many Oreo balls did you eat?"

"I dunno," murmured Ethan. "A lot."

Kit fought valiantly to keep the rising smile from his face, knowing Ethan would only cry more if he thought he was being laughed at.

"Why don't you go sit at the table and Uncle Basie will give you another?"

"Kit—" Lewie objected, but Kit had already sent him toddling back into the dining room. "His dinner is going to be completely ruined."

Kit shrugged. "There's always dinner tomorrow. It's a small price to pay to give you one less thing to worry about when you're already worked up."

"I'm not worked up!" Lewie snapped, sounding incredibly worked up.

Kit raised his eyebrow and waited.

They stared at each other for a long second, before Lewie swung his rag over his shoulder and tossed his hands out. "Orion's gone."

"Gone?" Kit sat up straighter.

"Not like, *gone* gone. But they've been having these walking stints, where they take Canis and their cane and just go…out. They were supposed to be home an hour ago. Now they're late to their own birthday dinner, and if they don't show up, it's really going to bum the kids out." Lewie rubbed the crease between his brows. "When it first started happening, I'd put all the kids in the car and just start driving around town looking for Ri, asking folks on the sidewalk if they'd seen them. How far could a single kid go with just their guide dog, you know? Pretty far, apparently.

I've grounded them, taken their phone away, and watched them like a hawk. I've done everything I'm supposed to, and they *still* manage to slip out the back door when no one is looking. All because I'm too busy worrying about literally everything else and I can't give a single teenager my full attention. I shouldn't *have* to."

"No, you definitely shouldn't." Kit padded closer to Lewie. He thought for a moment, then dropped his voice to a whisper. "Don't you have a way of—well, *knowing* where Orion is?"

It was a delicate question to ask, considering Lewie had never personally confirmed that there was a *knowing* in the first place. Since shaking Lewie's hand that first hot, summer day at Wellhead, Kit had suspected there was something *more* to Lewie. Then once, in bed beneath the cozy darkness of a winter night, Basie had confessed his own suspicions like they had been lying on his mind just as he lay across Kit's bare chest.

He always knows when he's about to get sent on a call five minutes before it comes from dispatch, he whispered. *And, when I was in Berkeley Springs, he knew the second I wanted to come back home. I mean, he literally called that minute. Do you think he's a mind reader?*

Kit didn't know any mind readers. Faeries, some. Immortals, plenty. But mind readers? He could only suppose if he *had* met a mind reader, they'd been kind enough to leave him in his ignorance.

So, Kit and Basie called it what the locals had been calling it all along, the Knowing. And Lewie, for all he trusted them with his children and all his other secrets, never confirmed nor denied its existence. Bringing it up now as a magical solution, so to speak, was playing dirty. But it was worth the mention if it meant keeping Orion safe and Lewie sane.

Lewie shifted uncomfortably. "It…doesn't work that way. If it did, this would've stopped being a problem months ago."

"Months?" asked Basie from the doorway, arms crossed over his chest. He slipped into the kitchen and gently rubbed Kit's back. It was something Basie always did when he was deep in thought, as if the touch completed a circuit that could both inspire and calm him. "Why didn't you call?"

The question made Lewie pull his phone out of his pocket, seemingly checking for any missed calls or messages. Off to his side, Kit could see the phone was completely empty of notifications. Just a picture of Lewie holding newborn Ethan and a time-stamp that exposed Orion as *late.*

"They don't answer their phone if they know I'm the one calling," Lewie said mindlessly.

"Not Rion, man. Call *us.* I'm out on the town all day for work. It's not a problem to give a quick drive around."

"It's not your mess, Basie."

Kit sensed danger as soon as the words hit the air, like a tangible change in the room. Maybe it was just the back door opening.

Then, Orion opened their godforsaken mouth.

"*Woooow.* Glad to know what you really think of me, Lew."

All eyes turned to the back door where Orion was kicking off a pair of muddy boots. Canis was close at their side, paws just as grubby, filth visible even on her brown fur.

"Nothing says brotherly love like your own brother calling you a fucking mess when he thinks you're not listening. Hell, let's take a fucking trip to Philly," they continued.

At first, no one said anything. Basie was glaring down Lewie, practically begging him to break the awkward silence, but Lewie only chewed on his lips, face red.

So, that left Kit.

"Happy birthday, Orion," he said. "Basie and I brought you pie and Oreo balls."

"Thanks, man. Guess you only have to live to a hundred to learn to have some goddamn manners. I'm glad you brought up the whole birthday thing, actually." Basie caught Kit's glance across the kitchen and shook his head. *Abort, abort.* "'Cause, get this, turning eighteen means I've aged out of the Lewie Simon Prison System. I'm not anyone's *mess* anymore. I'm a legal adult and that means I'm finally free of being grounded by my own brother, so happy fucking birthday to me."

"Are you done?" Lewie exclaimed, louder than he probably meant to.

The house went silent. Orion smiled.

"Yes, I'm done."

Lewie was a stick of dynamite with the fuse already creeping down the line.

"One: It's a really good thing you decided to show up, because your brothers and sisters spent all afternoon baking you a special birthday cake. You're pissed at me? Fine. But if you start taking that out on everyone else, we're going to have a serious problem."

"Why'd they bake a cake if Kit was just going to bring a pie? I don't even *like* sweets. And I fucking hate Oreos."

Basie's jaw dropped.

"*Two,*" Lewie continued through his teeth. "As long as you live in this house and—"

"Under your roof, what you say goes. Yeah, boss. No need to go all family sitcom on me. I got it."

"Do you? Because your ramble in the mud seems to suggest otherwise. I asked you to be here on time. I asked you to let me know where you'd be. I asked you to answer my calls."

Orion began untangling the dozen necklaces hanging from their throat, separating lockets from pendants, charms from beads. "There's a third thing on this list, isn't there?"

Lewie looked as though he very badly had something to say. But this wasn't the time or place to start unpacking whatever had crawled up into Orion's ass and died. Not when the younger kids could hear. Not with Kit and Basie in the room.

"No. Just sit down at the table and I'll make you a plate. We're going to have a nice family dinner if it kills us."

Kit fully expected Orion to slip their shoes back on and disappear back into the early autumn drizzle. But they only let go of Canis' harness and traipsed into the dining room, hand grazing the wall as they went.

There was a soul deep sigh that pushed out of Lewie's lips as he scrubbed his hands over his face. Basie came up behind him, giving his shoulder blades a friendly rub that was more rough than comforting.

"Come on, Lew. Let's eat."

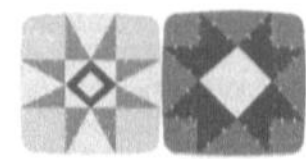

IT WAS THE QUIETEST birthday dinner Kit had ever attended, and he'd had a lot of birthdays.

The kids tossed glances around the table, gnawing on their skewers and waiting for either Orion or Lewie to say something. Since both refused to be the first to crack, that left the sound of cutlery scraping against the plates and Sam's frequent burps—a symptom of incurable gassiness he insisted was caused by too many vegetables on his plate.

This was how Kit knew it was bad. Lewie hadn't told him to say excuse me once, which seemed to only make Sam expel more air from the depths of his body.

"Can I throw out the rest of my vegetables?" Sam exclaimed, shattering the silence with a hammer.

"The ones I grew myself?" Basie remarked. "Absolutely not. You only have a few left. It won't kill you."

"How do you know? What happens if I blow up like a balloon from all the gas? All my internal organs will stop working and the doctors won't be able to fix me because I won't fit in the hospital and you'll have to tie me with string and send me off to the Macy's Thanksgiving Day Parade. And Thanksgiving isn't for another two months! Is that how you want to see me? Just once a year floating down a city street a million miles away."

"It's not a million miles," Eliza stated evenly, emboldened by her middle school education. "It's only two hundred."

"You're making that up," Sam accused.

"Am *not*. I did a project where I had to use a real map to measure the miles from Long Lily to a bunch of different cities. Los Angeles is over two thousand miles away. Philadelphia is a hundred. I got an A-plus. When was the last time *you* got an A-plus on anything?"

"Alright, cool it," Lewie warned.

"It'd be kinda awesome to have a brother in the Macy's Thanksgiving Day Parade," Tallie said. "Johnny at school once said his sister played trumpet in the parade, but I think it would be so much better if Sam got to be a balloon. You could see all the people watching." She popped a potato into her mouth, chewed thoughtfully, then added, "We could take a picture and put it on the Christmas cards. All of us could be holding a string. I bet you they'd turn that into a postcard at the post office."

"I think we're ignoring an important piece of information here," Basie interjected. "People don't turn into balloons."

"Do you have proof?" Meyer asked, peeling an onion off of his kebab. "If Santa can fit down our chimney and the tooth fairy can hold all those gross teeth in her tiny bag, why couldn't a person blow up into a balloon?"

From the seat next to him, Kit saw Orion open their mouth with a know-it-all kind of smirk. Kit could not know for certain what unfortunate thing they were about to say—if they were about to burst the kids' bubbles about Santa *and* the tooth fairy—but he did not want to find out. Before he could think twice, he grabbed Orion's wrist and squeezed.

"No, thank you," Kit stated seriously.

Orion snatched their hand away instantly.

"Didn't realize I'm not allowed to speak in my own house," they hissed quietly.

"You know that's not it. You were about to—"

"God, Kit, I'm an asshole, but I'm not that *cruel*. I thought you were the only person at this table who had my back."

"Of course I do—"

Sam slammed his hands on the table decisively. "I bet if we stretched people little by little, we could learn how to fill them up with air and then send them to the moon that way. You wouldn't need a rocket anymore."

"I once saw a lady blow up because she ate peanuts. That might work," Tallie suggested.

Orion scraped their fork on their plate painfully loud to yank back Kit's attention.

"You just think I'm an awful person because I don't like being told what to do," they continued furiously. Across the table, Basie took notice of their private conversation and scrunched his brows. Kit ignored him. The second Kit began to dispute the unfair accusation though, Orion was barreling on. "If I was going to be cruel, you'd know. Like this."

They sat up straighter and announced, "So, Basie, I hear you signed up to become a full-time firefighter with the LLFD."

The table went quiet.

Basie spun to Kit with a look of terror.

Kit thought his heart might be somewhere in the pit of his stomach, but he couldn't be sure. He wasn't certain what he was feeling. And somehow, even though the statement was about

Basie, everyone was looking at him.

Had they all known?

"Jesus Christ, Ri," Lewie mumbled.

"Oh, I'm so sorry," Orion continued sarcastically. "Kit, did you not know? I know you're a worrier, so I thought Basie would've told you right away—with how dangerous it is, and all. I mean, Lewie almost lost his leg once, and he's just a volunteer. But I didn't mean to spill the beans."

Shock gave way to anger, a heat in Kit's gut, boiling and boiling until it was at the top of his throat. He didn't know how to combat it, how he should react. Orion was itching for a reaction, that much was certain. He wouldn't let them have it, even if his voice shook. Even if he felt like he was going to be sick all over the shish kebabs.

"No apologies necessary, Ri. Of course I knew," Kit said steadily. The words came out as smooth and casual as they always did. He could tell his performance paid off when Orion's lips twitched down. "Basie's my husband. He tells me everything."

Basie met his eyes across the table and it was too much. A word began to tumble out of his mouth, so Kit stood to his feet as delicately as he could. Statistically speaking, nothing Basie said at this moment would stand a chance against…whatever this awful feeling was. Kit needed a few seconds to breathe. Possibly more than a few.

"I think we're ready for dessert," he said. "Lewie, is there still vanilla ice cream in the freezer? I think it'll go splendidly with the pie and the Oreo balls, even if some people at the table hate Oreos."

"Oh," Lewie sputtered. "Well, yeah sure. I'll go get—"

"No, I'll go," Kit rushed. "I know where it is."

"I'll go with you," Basie cut in. "There's, uh, a lot of ice cream to carry. A lot of hungry little faces."

Kit set his jaw, failing miserably to keep a grimace off his face, but nodded before fleeing into the kitchen. Basie was hot on his tail, but Kit was worried that if he didn't get a second to cool down and get his head on straight, he'd literally have a breakdown. He opened the freezer, letting the cool air rush over his hot face.

"Kit, honey…" Basie started quietly.

Kit spun around so quickly, his head began to swim. He held a hand up. He'd never had to draw a boundary like this before. Never felt so much *bad* with his husband that it staunched his ability to speak. But Basie understood. He backed off immediately.

"We're leaving after ice cream," Kit forced out. "You sit next to Orion."

"Okay. Whatever you want," Basie whispered shakily.

From the kitchen, Kit heard Orion say, "I don't understand why he's so upset. It's just a job change. It's not like Basie cheated on him."

It was *Sam,* of all children, who answered, "You never know when to shut up, do you?"

B ASIE DID NOT KNOW how badly he'd pissed off his husband. Kit had done an award-winning job at keeping his face frustratingly neutral, leaving Basie to dread the uncertainty of just how bad the damage was.

He didn't recommend pissing Kit off. In fact, if you were going to do a terrible thing, you might as well pick literally anything else and save yourself from The *Guilt*.

Very few people knew, because very few people were brave enough to do it, but inciting Kit's anger was a guarantee that you'd feel the ramifications of your actions down to the marrow of your bones. The only way to predict the resulting level of guilt was to imagine something worse than driving by a dog with a broken leg and not pulling over. Yanking a walker out from underneath a frail old lady named something sweet, like Frances or Eda. Waking up a child on Christmas morning, only to tell them Santa wasn't real and their stocking was full of coal. Or telling a guy you loved him and then fleeing town less than twenty-four hours later.

Oh, wait—Basie *had* done that one.

Right at this moment, though, he felt worse than if he'd done all of these things a hundred times over.

Basie's knuckles were bone white as he turned the van up

the driveway to Wellhead. In the passenger seat, Kit was still resolutely looking out the window, just as he had been since getting in the car. The flush that had burned Kit's face finally subsided. But with it went the rest of the color, leaving behind a pale, sickened expression that made Basie's stomach sour.

The drive back home had taken five minutes; had taken a century. Basie at least had the immortal wisdom to know better than to break the tense silence. Kit disliked arguing in the car just as much as he disliked arguing in front of other people. He'd wait until he crossed the cottage threshold before completely losing his head. But they were home now, so Basie was running out of seconds.

He threw the van into park. The second the locks perked up, Kit shoved out of his seat. He disappeared up the porch and through the front door in a flurry of long limbs and ruffled hair. Basie lingered with his hands on the wheel for a long, agonizing second.

Then, he went inside.

Kit hadn't even turned the lights on. He must've made a beeline straight to the kitchen, because when Basie slipped into the house, Kit was already at the counter, pouring himself a glass of wine. Red splotches splashed over the glass's edge as he brought it to his lips. He took his time drinking down the first two inches—the most gentleman-like chugging Basie had ever seen—before filling it up again.

Basie wasn't quite brave enough to leave the entryway, but he did muster enough grit to call down the hall, "I'm sorry I didn't tell you."

There. That was the most important part. If all else failed and if his explanations weren't enough, at least he'd said sorry.

"Are you?" Kit said finally, the first words he'd spoken since Lewie's kitchen. "Because it seems to me you're only sorry I found out the way I did."

"Well, I'm sorry for that too," Basie elaborated, twisting his hands. "I really had no idea the kids knew. They must've been eavesdropping when I called or gone through Lewie's texts or—I don't know. It doesn't matter. It was only supposed to stay between Lewie and me."

Kit scoffed, taking another hearty sip from his glass.

"No! No, that's not—" Basie hurried. "It was supposed to stay between Lewie, me, *and* you. But—"

"You couldn't be bothered to tell me." His tone betrayed the terrible cocktail of feelings he was trying to smother with the taste of his sweet wine. Kit placed his drink back on the counter with painful tenderness, almost as if he expected his anger had weakened the glass. That setting it on the counter too hard would send shards flying.

"To tell you the truth, I can't fathom what the hell you were thinking," Kit continued miserably. "On the drive home, I ran through all the reasons you possibly keep something like this from me. Dozens and dozens of possibilities, but not a single good one in the bunch. Not one that made any sort of sense. Then I started to wonder why I was so blessed *angry*. Husbands change jobs all the time, right? What should I care if mine is next on the list? It doesn't have anything to do with me." Kit pressed his lips together against a scowl, but it couldn't suppress his trembling. "But I *am* angry, Basie. I really could just strangle you."

He dug the heels of his hands into his eyes. "Not actually. I'd never lay my hands on you in violence. I feel I should say that."

"I know," assured Basie, cautiously easing his way down the hall like an alligator wrangler. "Wasn't worried you'd suddenly turn into a psychopath on me. And hey, look, you have every right to be angry. Just so long as you aren't angry forever."

"Not looking good," Kit mumbled, hands still pushing into his sockets.

To Basie's own terror, he couldn't tell if Kit was kidding or not. He waited on the other side of the kitchen island, letting the no man's land of maple wood and wine splashes protect them both from the crossfire. Up this close, it looked like the counter was the only thing keeping Kit on his feet.

"Okay, then talk to me," Basie begged, stretching his hand across the wooden surface. "I know you well enough to know that it's more than just—just *this.*"

Kit let out a shaky breath as a single tear escaped down the side of his freckled nose. He swiped it aside, rubbing harshly at his own cheek until the pale skin was raw and red.

"You know, for most of my life, I thought the only way I'd survive my immortality was by keeping record of the people I'd lost. I wrote it all down in a leather journal: their names, their favorite books, the good things they'd given me, the way they'd gone. I wrote a page for you when you left for Berkeley Springs, but I never truly resented you because it wasn't your fault. You'd lost your mother, you'd never left home, you *had* to go."

Kit threw his arms out at his sides with a mirthless laugh.

"But then you came back and I was the happiest I'd ever been. You appeared in that shed and I thought, *Here is the real Basie Yeats. It took a century, but here he is. How beautiful forever is going to be with this man.* But I guess…" Kit shook his head. "There will always be a part of you that cannot be predicted. It's the part of you that sold me this house. It's the part of you that whisked you out of state. And I'm *terrified* it'll be the part of you that wakes up one morning and realizes how—" He clutched his hands, searching for the right word. "—*simple* life is with me. I don't want to add you to that journal again."

Basie's heart dropped.

"What?" he said quietly.

"Have you considered that you didn't tell me about this because it would mean admitting you don't think we work as well as you thought?"

"Stop that!" Basie cried out, hands nearly coming up to cup his ears. This whole discussion was spiraling away from safe territory into a place he soon wouldn't be able to touch. "Quit—quit talking like that. Alright? You and I work just fine. Me making mistakes as your husband doesn't equate to you not being enough for me or something," Basie laid his hands flat on the counter, gazing so hard at his husband, Kit had no choice but to look back. "For the record, I *love* my life with you. When I was gone those six months, I was so miserable, it was all I knew how to be. I stand by my choice to be with you because you are the *best* thing to ever happen to me."

"Then why did you not bring up firefighting to me? Not once?"

"I didn't want to *worry* you, Kit!" Basie exclaimed.

Something flipped their magnets, because Basie had gone from needing at least three feet of distance from his husband to needing to be right there next to him. He circled round to Kit and clutched the untucked tails of Kit's button-down. Shame nearly kept Basie from peering up to Kit's eyes, knowing he'd find them bitterly glossy and red, but he did it anyway—just so Kit would know he meant what he was about to say. Kit's expression softened. His hand fell limply over Basie's, a sign that neither of them had thrown in the towel quite yet.

"I didn't want to worry you," Basie repeated. "That's the reason. It's a shitty one, I know. But I couldn't. Not until I knew it was a done deal. Not until there was anything real to worry about."

Basie kept his tone under control, pouring honesty onto the words until they were drenched with it. The effort it took to keep from spilling gasoline on this fight made Basie's hands shake. But it was worth it to keep it contained, still hovering in the realm of *We can fix this.*

"I signed up to worry about you," Kit said, finally. "It was kind of included in that whole marriage thing—you know, that sacred covenant we agreed to with all the wordy vows? I seem to remember something about honesty. *Trust.* Maybe I was at a different wedding than you were."

"You weren't," Basie promised. "All that wordy sacred vow stuff is right here."

He tapped over his heart.

"I think I might've taken it too seriously and made you think that I didn't care at all what you thought," Basie continued. "The truth is, I care way too much. I vowed to protect you and when I tried to, I had a spectacularly shitty way of going about it. I should've talked to you."

Kit pressed his lips together, eyes drifting over to the living room, where they'd hung Basie's favorite portrait from their wedding album.

"Basie, I didn't marry you so you could protect me from all the bad feelings of this world. I married you so that when things got hard, I could pull up your bootstraps and you could pull up mine, and we'd face our problems as a pair."

Basie dropped his head into Kit's chest, shaking his head. To his surprise, Kit let him.

"I just pictured you spending all day imagining a million different scenarios of how I could die. And if we're going to be around for a while, I didn't want that to be the way you lived," said Basie.

"I hate to break it to you, but I *have* been worrying. Your head has been everywhere except on your shoulders lately. I thought maybe your immortality sickness set in earlier than your mom's, or—" Kit looked away, unable to hide a wave of heartsickness. "God, I really, truly thought you were halfway out the door."

Basie looked up in a flash, the death grip on Kit's shirt even tighter.

"*No,*" he swore seriously. "That is the opposite of what I want. The opposite of what I was trying to do. I swear, I only kept it from you so it wouldn't….plague you, I guess. I was going to tell you as soon as I made up my mind. As soon as it was final."

"Orion said you were signed up. That sounds pretty final to me."

Basie let out a rushing sigh. In the heat of his own panic, he'd forgotten about Orion.

Knowing Orion had made their declaration with the intention of hurting Kit brought its own ache. Basie had been in the hospital waiting room with Lewie the day Orion was born. He attended Orion's mother's funeral, and then their father and stepmother's funeral. Eighteen years filled with babysitting stints, Spanish tutoring, and deep talks had given Orion the ammunition they needed to hurt Basie where it mattered.

"It's *almost* final," Basie said quietly.

"The only thing I don't understand is *why*," Kit said. "All of this came out of nowhere."

"I had been tossing the idea back and forth. At first, I thought the only reason I wanted to do it was because it was flashy and exciting, like when I moved to West Virginia. I thought that if I did a bit of research and rode the high of the possibility, that the rose-colored glasses would crack and I'd get over it. But I didn't. The more I started watching training videos and reading stories from first responders, the more I could picture myself in it. *I* was the one putting out the fires. *I* was the one doing CPR. Once I realized all that, I couldn't figure out how to tell you without scaring you. But I shouldn't have let that stop me from communicating with you and trusting you to be strong enough to handle it. I'm sorry."

With a gentleness that was so Kit-like, he nudged Basie back. At first, Basie dreaded that his explanation had been inadequate, useless in convincing Kit to forgive him. But then Kit hopped up onto the counter and tugged Basie into the space between his legs. His face was still hard, but he'd begun to run his fingers through Basie's curls, which was promising.

"You said it's nearly final?" Kit murmured.

"The paperwork is handed in and I passed the written exam. Flying colors."

This news didn't seem to surprise Kit.

"What's left?"

"The Fire Academy. It's a fourteen-week program in Harrisburg."

Kit's frown deepened. "That's an hour away."

"I don't mind the drive," Basie said with a light shrug. "They'll test me once a week. Not everyone makes it. If I can't get my gear on fast enough or do enough jumping jacks, they'll give me the boot." He let out a mirthless chuckle. "Who knows? Maybe I'll be home after a few days."

"You'll pass," Kit said with easy certainty. The anger had begun to seep out of his voice, leaving behind a man who was exhausted. But a man who was also made of strength and dependability. "Four months is a long time to be away from home."

"It is. That's why I'm commuting. I know we have plenty of time, but I don't want to waste any away from you."

"Basie, they're going to start early in the morning. You'll have to be on the road by 5 a.m.."

"Then I'll go to bed early. It'll be nice to tuck in at the same time as you for once."

Kit's lips pressed together in consideration, throat bobbing. Even though the sting of their argument was fading, he still smiled softly. Basie was up to his throat in love.

"You really want to be a firefighter?" Kit asked.

"I've been an electrician for *sixty years*. I've loved my job—I have—but it's the only thing I've ever done. I'm ready to do something for the community. Something more than just selling used books at the library and doing free electric fixes. I mean, who's better for the LLFD than someone who *knows* this town?"

"You've got a point," Kit agreed softly. Basie smiled, unconsciously fumbling with one of the buttons on Kit's shirt.

"The timing *feels* right, Kit. My boss says my apprentice is doing great. She's more than ready to take over for me." He tugged on the button until it almost snapped, before realizing all of his excitement was funneling through his fingers. He wiped his palms on his pants to expel some of the energy.

"I've really thought this through. Lewie and I have talked about it nonstop for the last few months. Not because I trust him more," Basie rushed out, grabbing Kit's knees. "But because he's lived it. It's not always glamorous heroics, and he made sure I knew that. Even with all the hard things, I really think it's what I'm meant to do. I want to try."

Basie guided Kit's thighs until they were brushing up against his sides, cradling him. Kit's silence was making his nerves run overtime, so Basie prodded, "How do you feel about it? I mean, how do you *really* feel about it? I know what I said, but I love you more than any new job I could possibly have. If you despise this idea, I don't have to go to the Academy. I can keep being the Long Lily Electrician if it gives you peace of mind. I wouldn't fault you for wanting that. You married an electrician. That's what you signed up for."

Brown eyes molten with affection, Kit stroked Basie's cheek with the back of his fingers. Even with the echoes of the fight still resonating between them, the featherlight touch brought chills up Basie's spine.

"No, sweetheart, I married Basie Yeats, who happened to be an electrician. Now he's going to be a firefighter." Basie's face lit up. He folded his hands over Kit's and squeezed. "Go to the Fire

Academy, Basie."

"Really?" asked Basie hopefully. "Doesn't it scare you?"

"It scares the breath out of me," Kit confessed. "But that's something we can handle together. I'm a century old. I've lived through some of the most terrifying moments of history, but I never let them get in the way of good things. You becoming a firefighter is a grand idea."

Basie felt like he was hearing things. Maybe he'd given up on the fight ending like this when everything exploded out of his control, but here it was. A glimmer of goodness in the aftermath of the wreckage.

"Does that mean I have your blessing?" Basie pressed hopefully.

"You have my insistence, you aggravating bastard," said Kit, laughing as Basie enveloped himself into his arms.

The embrace left no room for air. No room for seeds of distrust or uncertainty to grow. How could there be, when Kit's warmth was the steadiest thing Basie knew? He didn't realize he was crying until he felt each of his silent tears bloom into wet spots as they landed on Kit's shirt beneath his cheek. Neither of them cared. There was only the relief of the wide-open future and the surety that came when they held each other in the dark.

"We're okay?" Basie murmured into Kit's tear-soaked shoulder.

"We're okay." Kit pulled back and brushed his thumbs over Basie's damp face. "But if you *ever* keep something like this from me again, we won't be."

Unable to trust his voice, Basie nodded.

They stared at each other for a long moment, and it occurred to Basie that sometimes he wished he really could live forever.

That immortality sickness wouldn't eventually take away the one thing they were promised. He wanted to fill up his endless life with moments like this and never have to give them up. It made him understand why Kit was so scared of sending Basie off into the fiery unknown, but it also made Basie understand why Kit agreed that this was something Basie had to do. They *wouldn't* live forever, but the near reality of it was in their hands. Something to mold and shape and cherish. Something to boldly trust.

Leaning toward to brush a kiss on Basie's cheek, Kit said, "Got any of those Oreo balls left?"

Basie blinked, before scanning the kitchen counters. Next to the stove, the last few of Basie's Oreo balls waited under crinkled plastic wrap. He brought the bowl between them, letting Kit take the first pick before plucking his own. Kit tapped his confection against Basie's.

"*Sláinte*," said Kit, smiling for the first time in what seemed like hours.

"*Salud,*" laughed Basie.

Basie popped the entire thing into his mouth the same time Kit did. It didn't compare to the very first one he'd eaten hours ago, and the five or six he'd eaten since then had dulled the deliciousness-factor. But watching the delighted surprise pass over Kit's expression made it even sweeter.

"Definitely not as good as my pie," Kit appraised with a teasing grin. "But a nice start."

"A nice—" Basie scoffed. "You're lucky I owe you big time and let you win."

"*Uh huh.* Sure, Bas."

Then, before Basie could argue anymore, Kit wrapped his arms back around Basie and tugged him in for a kiss.

Just one brush of lips from the man he'd been married to for a full year and Basie felt just as melty as one of his confections. When Kit pulled away, he licked his bottom lip with a pleased little smile.

"You had a little chocolate," Kit said, tapping the corner of Basie's mouth. "Just there."

"Well," Basie crooned, draping his arms around Kit's shoulders. "I hate to tell you, baby, but you're a mess. I mean, you're just *covered* in chocolate."

Basie was already kissing Kit's smile when his husband rumbled another deep laugh and dropped his hands into Basie's back pockets.

"How kind of you to help me," he murmured against Basie's lips. "But maybe you should do a more thorough check upstairs?"

One thing was true: if Kit was terrible at flirting, Basie was even worse.

"You're lucky, sir. Most folks have to dial 911 before getting such *thorough* aid."

Kit groaned. "Is that what this is? Firefighter Basie to my rescue? *Oh no, I can't breathe; if only there was a sexy firefighter to save me.* Is that how it's going to be from now on?"

Basie was already halfway down the hall to the stairs. He stopped at the first step, leaning over the banister to keep an eye on Kit, only to get stuck tugging his shirt up over his head.

"Until the real thing ruins it for me forever? Absolutely." He yanked the shirt off and whipped it over his shoulder. "So…are you comin' or what?"

Kit gave a half-hearted shrug. "I've passed out from CO2

exposure and can't move."

Then, because he was a little shit, Kit held his arms out in a *pick-me-up* fashion. Basie stomped back down the hallway and did his very best, uneducated attempt at a firefighter's lift, hoisting his lanky patient over one shoulder. A positively delightful squeal flew out of Kit, who clung to Basie's waist for dear life.

"Good god," Kit gasped, fingers digging into Basie's shirt. "Definitely going to pass those strength tests."

At the top of the steps, Basie let Kit to his feet, unbuttoning Kit's shirt as soon as he stood upright. Basie kissed him again, heat under his lips and on the breath.

"Give me twenty minutes and I'll show you what other tests I can ace."

It was forty—and he did.

O RION SIMON COULDN'T TELL you what the fuck was going on.

They couldn't tell you what was going on with themself, that is. Rion could talk your ear off about literally anything else. In just one breath, Orion was prone to telling you about the genuinely concerning state of the government, the fine art of spinning honey, and the eight billion things their oldest brother had done that morning to piss them off.

But if a judge sat Orion down in a courtroom, made them swear on a holy book, and asked them, *"Orion Simon, do you or do you not know what the* fuck *is going on with you?"* then Orion wouldn't have an answer and…Well, the jury finds the defendant guilty, your honor.

Luckily, they weren't in a courtroom. Rion didn't think jail would be particularly kind to a nonbinary blind person. Though, Rion didn't think jail was kind to anybody. That was kind of the whole point.

Orion's current situation was worse than all that. Explaining themself to an uppity judge they'd never have to encounter again was one thing. It was another thing when the recipient of their worthless explanations and apologies was Kit Elliot. Orion just might prefer to volunteer for a life sentence rather than confront

Kit, who was the least awful person they had ever met. Even Basie was a little shit some of the time.

Too late to do anything about it now.

Orion felt Lewie's truck roll to a stop. His brother shifted gears down drive, past neutral and manual, into park—clickclickclick. If Orion hadn't been warned about their destination, they still would've known where they were based on the short drive and the distinct feeling that seeped in through a crack in the window—that same call to restful ease that suffused the Wellhead property.

"Well?" Lewie said. "Go on. Get."

For some reason, Lewie's Appalachian accent was always at its peak when he was herding Orion. Even worse, Orion's own mountain twang sometimes reared up when they were bitching back. It was nothing compared to what Orion had heard further south, but it was there.

"If you're worried about Basie, he's at work," Lewie continued.

Orion knew that. Orion knew the location of everything and everyone with faultless precision. That was their Knowing.

And Orion Knew that Kit Elliot was currently located in his kitchen. His *exact* location was a bit more difficult to pinpoint. Orion couldn't *picture* Kit's location exactly—they couldn't visually picture much of anything. Instead, the answer to *Where is Kit Elliot?* came in words.

The answer shifted from **north kitchen** to **south kitchen** to **the sink** to **three feet in the air** in dizzying succession. Sometimes it twirled too quickly for Orion to gauge the answer. Sometimes it...lowered? Dipped?

"I think he's *dancing*," Orion blurted.

"Basie?"

"No, dumbass. *Kit.*"

"How on earth could you possibly know that?"

"Well you see, long ago, our great-great-great-great grandfather—"

"As much as I love rehashing old family legends, the sooner you get your groveling in, the sooner we can go home."

Sometimes, Lewie was right. Statistically, it had to happen eventually. ▫

"Maybe I should wait a minute. If I go in now, I'm only going to embarrass him."

Lewie scoffed, tapping the steering wheel in the way that was part of his annoying brother brand. "Didn't know you cared, considering you've already gone out of your way to humiliate him once."

Well, that settled it. It seemed Orion was always choosing one unpleasant thing over another. Right at this moment, they'd do just about anything to get out of this goddamned truck—even if it meant admitting for the first time in recorded history that they were wrong.

Orion pressed the buckle and let themself out, before yanking the back door open to let Canis free from the cab. She leapt directly to Orion's side.

"Harness up," Rion commanded. Canis' paws scraped the gravel of the driveway as she shifted into place. When she was facing the right way, Rion lowered the harness onto Canis' back.

"I'll wait here for you," Lewie called. "Remember—"

Orion slammed the door.

Walking up the Wellhead drive was as familiar as walking up the path to their own house, even if it was a march of shame. Canis remained faithfully at Rion's side, coming to a halt at the base of the porch. This was usually the time Orion would give Canis a harness command to find the railing, but Orion had been to Wellhead enough times to know how to find it and get to the front door without help.

Orion could hear music on the other side. They paused, frowning. Not just any music. *Abba.* It was loud enough to blare through the old walls of the cottage, resounding through the door to where Orion was hesitating. They pressed the doorbell, holding it long enough to hopefully give it a fighting chance of being heard over the Swedish pop music.

Nothin'.

Orion pressed the doorbell again. When no one answered, they asked into the radio silence of their mind: *Where is Kit Elliot?*

In the kitchen—still dancing.

With a sigh, Orion fished their necklace of keys from beneath their t-shirt. The necklace must have looked wild to sighted people, but Orion liked it for the sound it made when they walked and the way it felt to touch, fidget with when they were anxious. The feeling of a dozen keys on separate chains jangled around over their heart, along their collarbone. Most of the keys were non-functional; ones Orion had gotten from asking, *Where is the nearest forgotten key?* But their own house key was in there, and the Wellhead one too. That was the one they reached into the spiderweb of chains for, asking a silent, *Where is the Wellhead key?*

Just on the other side of your thumb.

Orion plucked it out.

This was one of Orion's parlor tricks. The reaction they got from able-bodied people was always the same: *My, how did that poor visually impaired child know exactly what key goes to the right house?*

Ugh, gag.

They actually didn't end up needing the key, though. Kit had left the house open—again. It seemed he always left the house open when he was still home because he did not believe Long Lily had robbers or vandals. Who knew? Maybe it didn't.

Giving their shoulders a little shake, Orion let themself inside. The assault on their ears was immediate.

"Dooon't go wasting your emoooo-tion! Lay all your love on meeee."

Kit Elliot could do a lot of things, but—God bless him—he could not sing.

Orion couldn't think of a good way to interrupt the song. They hoped to come up with something genius to say on the way from the entryway down the hall to the kitchen, but inspiration never struck. That left them standing right at the long carpet's edge, Blair Witching in the doorway. They had half a mind to give a little *knock knock knock* on whatever hard surface was closest, but—

"—devoooo-AH!"

Something Kit-sized slammed into the counter with an ungraceful *thud*. Orion gnawed on the inside of their cheek while they waited for Kit to get his gasping breaths in check.

"You scared the daylights out of me," Kit heaved in laughter, voice coming out muffled, as if he were holding his hands over his face. "I'm telling Basie to take away that spare key."

"The door was open," Orion pointed out. They wrapped their hand around all their necklaces and shook them. "'Sides, you'd have to find it first."

There was an awkward silence, like Kit was remembering that he wasn't thrilled with Orion at the moment. Orion had never known how to fill silences, because sometimes it was hard to tell what was happening in them. Sometimes they read the room wrong and reacted strangely, which usually resulted in a disastrous quiet that was even heavier with tension than before. A monumental ultra-silence.

Orion felt a hand land gently on their wrist.

"Come sit down. Stay a while," said Kit. "Basie's out on an electrical call. Someone rode their dirt bike into a telephone pole."

"Heard about that," Rion answered, taking a seat at the table. "The call came over the radio. Lewie said the guy who was driving is alright."

Orion heard the sound of a chair scraping across the floor as Kit took a seat opposite them.

"That's great," said Kit, and it seemed like he really meant it. "Must be strange to be the first to learn about emergencies."

The room went silent. Without the cushion of small talk between them, Kit and Orion seemed to be acknowledging the unspoken understanding that Orion was here to apologize and still hadn't gotten around to actually doing it. Or, at least, Orion supposed Kit knew what this house call was about. They wouldn't have been here otherwise. They only hoped Kit wouldn't ask the dreaded question.

Kit asked anyway.

"What's going on with you, Orion?"

The jury finds the defendant…

"I'm sorry I told you Basie's news," Rion said instead of answering. "He wasn't keeping it from you. I mean, he was. But I had heard him on the phone with Lewie. He had literally just signed up an hour before you came over. I'm sure he would've talked to you after dinner. So uh, yeah. I'm a piece of shit."

"You're not," Kit promised, laying his fingers gently over the back of Orion's wrist. "*I'm* sorry you overheard our conversation with your brother. It was rude to talk about you behind your back, especially where you could hear."

"It's not talking behind my back if it's right. I mean, I have been wandering."

Kit withdrew his touch, almost like he needed both hands in order to fold them together thoughtfully. It seemed like an old-man habit a person like him might have.

"Would you like to tell me why?"

They felt their brain go into overdrive, scrounging around for anything that could distract them from how this conversation made their skin feel like it was about to peel off. The soapy scent in the air from the dishes. The low rumble of Abba turned all the way down to the lowest volume. Canis at their side, head laying across Orion's boots.

"Do I have to?" they asked, finally.

"Of course not. I only thought it might be nice for you to have someone to talk to who wasn't directly related to you."

Orion sighed in relief. So not an interrogation, then.

"It would be," Rion agreed. "But I can't."

Don't ask why. Don't ask why. Don't ask why.

"Alright. I understand," Kit agreed calmly.

That was it? Orion felt their jaw drop, literally drop, and Kit laughed.

"What, did you think the immortal man with a century-old secret would be the one to start nosing around in your business?"

"Basie does it all the time."

"Basie has severe—oh, what is it called? MOMA?"

Orion cringed. "FOMO? 'Fear of missing out'?"

"Yes, that. Part of me thinks it's half the reason he signed up for the Fire Academy. He wants to be involved. He wants to help."

"Can I ask you something?" Orion said, scratching the back of Canis' head. Kit hummed in reply. "Why were you so upset about Basie becoming a firefighter?"

"It's complicated. I was embarrassed, I think. And upset that he'd made such a significant decision without talking to me at all. But I reacted so strongly because…" A thoughtful silence. "Well, aren't you a little scared every time Lewie gets sent on a call?"

Orion's insides felt like one of those car crumple zones—those places where they drive cars into brick walls on purpose. Canis' head rose from Orion's feet, sensing something was off.

And then—a miracle.

From the driveway, Lewie's monstrosity of a truck let out two loud *HONKS*.

Orion was grabbing the dog's harness and jolting out of the chair before Kit could say anything else.

"You and Basie left last night before we could cut the cake," they said. "It's awful. I don't know what those children did to that box cake mix, but if you want a slice, we brought you one. It's in the truck. Lew is waiting for me."

"Oh, uh, alright then. I'll follow you out. Thank you."

Orion took down the hall, letting Canis take the lead even though they knew exactly where they were going.

"You know," Kit said, following behind, "you and Basie react exactly the same when I go digging where you don't want me to. You're practically twins. Same brooding."

Orion paused and turned over their shoulder in Kit's direction.

"If I were like Basie, Lewie might like me more," they said, then stormed off.

Kit seemed to pause behind Orion, and then jogged to catch up.

When they got to the truck, Orion knocked on the side of the truck and heard Lewie roll the window down. Lewie placed the cake into their waiting hands, but didn't say anything. Things weren't going horribly with Kit, and they wanted to keep it that way—they could deal with their brother later. A second later, Orion handed off the Saran-sealed plate to Kit, who accepted it as if it were a rare treasure.

"I know you've been baking for a hundred years, but don't be too hard on that poor cake. It didn't choose the life it leads." They inhaled sharply, but somehow still couldn't get enough air. Their lungs still felt half-empty when they said, "And, Kit? Sorry. Again."

Orion half expected Kit to spiral into another round of *No, I'm the one that's sorry.* But that wasn't what he answered—not at all.

With so much tenderness it made Orion's throat close, Kit laid his hand on their shoulder and said, "You are exactly where you're supposed to be, Orion Simon."

And that was the worst part—knowing Kit was right, but not knowing what the hell to do with it.

When they got home, Orion walked straight through the house, unlatched the back door, and wandered.

September, 2025

B ASIE WAS MAN ENOUGH to admit that he'd gotten a little too competitive over dessert at Orion's birthday those few months ago.

He was not proud of the way he coerced Lewie's siblings and called the man he married maggot food. Kit, the light of Basie's hearth and home, was anything *but* maggot food. Henceforth, Basie had resolved to treat him as such. No more rivalries with his husband.

But Jacob Phillips was not Basie's husband. He was just the arrogant homophobe who happened to attend the Fire Academy with Basie. So, Basie would do whatever it took to smear that snotty asshole's face into the gritty parking lot of their training grounds until Jacob's blood ran black as asphalt. Then, for the satisfaction of it all, Basie would do it again. That's what the Lord meant when he said *turn the other cheek*, right?

Of course, this was all metaphorical. Basie would lose his job if he *actually* made Jacob Phillips bleed, and he'd spent too many days driving back and forth to Harrisburg to let it all go to waste now. His actual plan of attack had less to do with bodily harm and more to do with outranking Phillips during all their tests. And so far? Basie was knocking it out of the fucking park.

He just had to get into his goddamn bunker gear in less than ninety seconds.

It had started like this: Captain Marsh had pulled Basie aside to tell him what an *extraordinary* job he was doing.

"Really, we haven't had a recruit pick everything up so quickly in a decade. The other guys oughta keep an eye on you and learn a thing or two. Keep up the good work, Butler."

That was what they'd decided to call him—an annoying play on William Butler Yeats, even though Basie already had three perfectly acceptable names. The compliment had been so satisfying, though, Basie couldn't find it in him to be peeved. He floated around the training base on a cloud, Number One Badass Recruit.

But then, the enemy.

"Gotta hand it to you, Butler," Jacob sneered later that day. *"You're doing alright for a gay guy. I still get into my bunker gear thirty seconds faster, though."*

And so, Basie had no choice: he would have to shave *forty-five* seconds off of his own record, even if it killed him.

Here and now, in his own living room with the furniture pushed aside, it just might.

Basie stared down at the pile of practice gear he'd swiped, scrunching his nose at the pristine, *new* smell it had. The fresh gear smell at least meant it was free from the chemicals and toxins a firefighter might encounter in the field. Everything was ready in grabbing order—from the standard trousers and jacket, to the boots and hand protection. The tiny pieces that posed the greatest challenge were there too. The flash hood, the hearing protection, even the goggles.

He drew in a deep breath through a small opening in his

lips and imagined his mark. "One minute, twenty-five seconds. That's all. One minute, twenty-five seconds. You got this, Butler," he told himself.

The clock struck four and Basie began to move like if he didn't get his butt into that gear right that second, it'd be the end of life as he knew it.

Good thing it wasn't. By the time everything was on, it had been a whopping two minutes and thirteen seconds.

Basie smacked his face in frustration. He was supposed to be getting better, not worse.

Grumbling, he stripped everything off and laid it back out, then tried again. And again. And again. And again, until Basie forgot a world before bunker gear.

His best time? One minute and thirty seconds—*exactly* Phillips' record. And he'd only been able to do it once. Basie took everything off and let his knees give out, tumbling to the floor in a heap.

"Is this a new firefighting technique I haven't heard of?" asked a familiar voice from the doorway. Basie tilted his head back until he was looking at Kit upside down. "The firefighter puddle?"

Back when he'd first started falling in love with Kit, he'd been surprised that the sight of a tall, redheaded man in pleated sand-colored pants could do it for him. Now, all the blood was rushing to his brain just so he could linger in the glorious vision a few moments longer.

"This isn't a technique. This is the precursor to a white flag. Surrender is coming any second now."

Kit's footsteps were soundless as he crossed the room. He settled at Basie's side, sitting on the only free patch of floor where there wasn't some type of protective equipment or another.

"It's not the end of the world if you get your gear on a *little* bit slower than Jacob Phillips, you know," Kit said. "It only counts during the real thing. Maybe once the sirens go off, he'll be shaking in his boots too much to even slide them on."

It was highly likely that Kit thought Basie was having another moment of unreasonable competitiveness, but that was only because Basie had left Jacob's homophobic remarks out when he recounted the story. Kit was already worried enough about Basie joining the LLFD. Basie wasn't going to let some asshat from Goldsboro make it worse.

"As much I appreciate what you're trying to do, I don't need comfort, I need a swift kick. Or a fire under my ass. Or—I don't know, I need better motivation," groaned Basie, laying his arm over his eyes. "Once I get the gear on, then I get to move onto the easier step: CPR."

"Is that what the pillows are for?"

This was in reference to all of the pillows from their bed, stacked neatly in a tall pile. Someone at the academy had told him more pillows were better than less, because real CPR had to go deep enough to potentially crack a few ribs.

"Hey, those pillows symbolize a dying person with a name."

"My apologies, I haven't made their acquaintance. They're called..."

"John Doe. The victim didn't have ID on him when we arrived on the scene."

"I see," hummed Kit, amused. "Better get to work saving John Doe, then."

With that, Kit lay completely flat with his back to the floor.

Before Basie could reason out what the hell he was doing, Kit grabbed the stack by the bottom pillow and laid it across his chest.

"Your gear isn't going to get itself on," Kit said—no, *flirted*.

Basie blinked. What could Kit *possibly* have to flirt about? This was just putting the gear on, a few chest compressions, a few rescue breaths, and then undressing out of the—

Oh. Yeah. Okay. He got it now.

Talk about motivation.

This time, when the second hand passed twelve, Basie was in his bunker gear in a minute, twenty-seven seconds. He dropped to Kit's side, folding his hands one on top of the other, before pressing the heel into the pillow stack in thirty perfect chest compressions. Then, he tilted Kit's head up, pinched his nose, and blew a long rescue breath into his mouth. On the second one, Kit's mouth drew closed, his hand cupping the back of Basie's head to give him a soft kiss.

Basie pulled back, a paper-thin space between them.

"This is supposed to be serious," he scolded without heat.

"A reward for a job well done *is* serious. Besides I'm the one that's dying, so we better..." Kit said, then closed the distance again.

Basie melted into the kiss, mindlessly pushing aside the pillows to make room. It was gentle, but there were still fingers in the curls at the nape of his neck, an arm wrapped tight around his back. Basie wanted to linger there forever, tasting the fresh oranges Kit had as a snack and letting the kiss make him dizzy. He stopped himself right before he could straddle the welcoming space on Kit's waist, pulling back abruptly.

"Oh my god, I let you seduce me," Basie accused.

"Nice to know I still can."

"Not right this second, it isn't! This is important." Basie shoved the pillows back onto Kit's chest. "No more funny business, sir. Or else I'll go give rescue breaths to another John Doe and he can watch me strip out of my bunker gear."

"For starters, it's not stripping if you're completely dressed underneath. Also, you *just* said we were eliminating the sexiness factor."

"I have to have a *little* bit of sexiness. Otherwise, how else will I end up in that calendar?"

"You know what, Bas?" Kit looked him up and down, assuming the John Doe position once more. "I wouldn't worry about that."

I f Orion had known how entertaining it would be, they wouldn't have shown up fifteen fashionable minutes late to this electrical safety Q&A. They'd expected to sink into one of the community center's uncomfortable plastic chairs and fall asleep to dumb questions that could be answered with a half-assed internet search. The event had drawn a crowd of locals who did not have friends, and therefore needed to get their daily dose of human interaction where they could.

So here was Orion Simon, Kit Elliot-Yeats (probably wearing his proudest *supportive husband* face), and ten of Long Lily's strangest inhabitants.

At the front of the room was probationary firefighter Basie Elliot-Yeats. When Basie had made it through the Fire Academy, he'd returned to Long Lily broadcasting that he'd graduated top of his class—and yes, he *had* put Jacob Phillips in his place. No one quite knew what that last bit was about, but they were happy for him, nonetheless.

Even Orion was a little proud. They expected Basie to jump right in, saving cats from trees and putting out wildfires.

This was…not that.

At this point in the Q&A, Basie had answered every manner of ludicrous question involving outlets wires, electrical breakers, and space heaters. Things like, *Can I run three hair dryers at once in my guest bathroom?* To which, Basie had replied, *What could you possibly need three hair dryers for?* The man harrumphed indignantly and said, *Wouldn't you like to know?*

(Kit had leaned over to Orion so they didn't miss the punchline. Apparently, Hair Dryer Man was *bald*—as smooth as a baby's bottom all over his scalp. Orion had half a mind to stand up and say *No no, what <u>do</u> you need three hair dryers for?* But some things are better left unsaid.)

The absurdity didn't end there. Orion's personal favorite question had been halfway through the session when a feeble-voiced old lady got off the shuttle from her nursing home, slowly inched her way up the center aisle, and whispered a question in Basie's ear. Orion didn't hear exactly what she asked, but Basie's answer had been telling enough: *I'm so sorry for the loss of your guinea pig, but no, you shouldn't try to create a defibrillator by running raw wires out of your outlets. You could get severely injured, and Bacon is probably already with the Lord.*

"Did you come just to laugh at your neighbors?" Kit asked as Orion gnawed on their knuckles to keep from chuckling.

"Of course not. I heard this was Basie's first outing as a fire-fighter. Wanted to come and offer my support. The laughing is just an added bonus."

"Uh huh," Kit deadpanned quietly into their ear. "If you say so."

Orion wiped their ear like Kit had spit into it.

"I needed out of that damn house, alright? And this is the only place I could go that wouldn't cause Lewis Simon to have a fatal conniption. He'll say, *Where were you Orion, you awful misfit thing?*

And I'll say, *I was just at the community center learning the importance of electrical safety.* And he'll say, *No the hell you weren't.* And I'll say, *Yes the hell I was, just ask Kit and Basie.* And *those,* my friend, are the magic words." Orion shrugged with one shoulder. "Plus, I never apologized to Basie for what happened at my birthday dinner. Two birds, one well thrown stone."

"I'll be your alibi, but you can't dance around your brother forever," Kit said, nudging Orion's elbow with his own.

"Says the guy who'll be *alive* forever."

"I'm only saying that—"

"Why do you care so much?" Orion turned to Kit, the way they'd learned as a child to make conversation more comfortable for sighted people. To Orion, though, Kit was just a blur of light and shadows. "I'm the opposite of your problem."

"Orion Simon!" Basie snapped from somewhere at the front of the room. "Shut your trap and quit hassling my husband. There's important information to cover, and I've only got thirty minutes to get through it all."

Orion sat forward, slinking like a shadow down into their seat with their arms crossed.

They made a silent vow to be quiet for the rest of the talk, which lasted... all of two minutes. Their fingers slipped underneath one of the keys on their stockpile of necklaces, fidgeting with the toothy edge and pressing indentations into their fingertips.

"Is he wearing the firefighter getup?" Orion whispered over to Kit.

"Indeed, he is," answered Kit, voice low with way too much interested heat. He might as well have said, *I want to strip that beautiful, beautiful man right out of that bunker gear and put out his fire.*

The corner of Orion's lip curled down. "Gross."

Maybe they'd try that quiet thing again.

Basie's timer warned there were five minutes left in the talk, and yet Orion hadn't heard a single worthwhile piece of information.

"Any more questions?" Basie pleased, sounding a little winded. "Anything *practical?*"

Silence echoed across the room.

Then Basie sighed and said, "Yes, Mr. Elliot?"

"It's Mr. Elliot-Yeats, actually."

Orion could feel Kit glowing with smirky satisfaction from their own seat.

"Or, for the love of—" Basie started, but Kit spoke over him.

"How do I know if I have a faulty outlet?"

Orion suspected that Kit already knew the answer—he'd married someone who'd been an electrician for over sixty years—but the question seemed to come as a welcome change for Basie.

"Oh!" he chirped, surprised. "That's an excellent question. A faulty outlet will have a bad smell, excess heat, or melted plastic. And with that reasonable question…" *Whap,* a notebook being slammed closed. "I'm calling this session over now. Remember people, if a firefighter wouldn't do it, *you* shouldn't do it."

Miffed grumbles and the scraping of chairs filled the room as Basie's humble audience rose to get back to their daily lives—the bald man retreating to his hair dryers and the old woman returning to mourning Bacon the guinea pig. Orion stretched their legs out in front of them like a cat after a long nap.

"Thank God. I could feel my brain cells slowly giving up hope," they said lethargically. With a slap on their knees, they stood up and reached for Canis' harness. "Well, Christopher, I think I have fulfilled my obligations as dutiful nibling. I hope Basie appreciates the hour of my life that I won't ever get back."

"Surely you're not talking about the hour you were supposed to be in school, are you?" came Basie's scolding tone from the side.

Orion scowled. Basie's hand dropped onto Orion's shoulder with a hearty squeeze, sending a startled jolt up their spine. They hated when people touched them without permission. At the very least, a little warning would be nice.

"Lewie used to cut class all the time his senior year. If you're starting your rebellious *Viva La Liberté* phase, there are more interesting things you can do than attend fire safety Q&As," continued Basie.

"Remind me never to do anything nice for you ever again," Orion grumbled. "How are you so sure I'm skipping class, anyway? For all you know, it's an in-service day and all my teachers are sitting in a circle singing campfire songs. I bet Mrs. Donlevy sings a mean 'She'll Be Comin' Round the Mountain.'"

Basie scoffed. "How do you *think* I know you're cutting class?"

All at once, a feeling of dread settled in Orion's gut.

"The jailer," they said in low realization. "Lewie texted you."

A set of footsteps approached with a familiar weighty gait. Canis, with no one holding her harness and therefore not in Work Mode, brushed past Orion to stroll up to greet the newcomer.

"Next time, I'll file a missing person's report," said Lewie dryly.

Orion squeezed their eyes shut. *Great day in the motherfucking morning.*

"I have an alibi," Orion said, holding their hands up in surrender. "He's six foot tall, a hundred and three years old, has awful taste in men, and had eyes on me the whole time."

"When you say it like that, it sounds like a crime," Kit chimed in, coming up to stand at Orion's shoulder. "But they were here the whole time, Lew. Basie only had to yell at them once."

Lewie was quiet for a moment. He always went quiet when he was doing mental gymnastics in order to catch Orion in some lie that, no matter how hard he tried, wouldn't exist. Lewie seemed to find it impossible that Orion could exist outside of his control without doing something unsavory. Orion had heard it all before, accused of buying drugs from untrustworthy sellers and drinking in the witching hours with friends they didn't have. Orion had tried to tell Lewie that they were just walking, and if he trusted them just once, he'd see that Orion was telling the truth. That was why Lewie was so stunned now, because Orion had an alibi and Lewie had no choice but to accept their explanation.

Still, Orion bolstered themself against whatever accusation Lewie would pull out of his pocket. They reached out for Canis, letting her slip her harness under their waiting fingers. Her soft coat brushing against their jeans steadied Orion, helping them keep their cool.

"If you skip class, you'll fall behind and risk retaking the year," Lewie stated, frustration dripping from every word. "Don't ask me how I know."

But Orion wanted to. Sometimes they wanted to hear about the Lewie that cut class and had to repeat senior year, because it would help them remember a version of their brother that did not drag around the ball and chain of seven children. Orion had been very young, but they still remembered Lewie as a teenager who craved fun and excitement. A teenager who, when he spoke cruelly to Orion, it had more to do with teenage angst and not his low opinion of Orion. Now, all Lewie knew how to be was a single parent with the world's largest stick up his ass.

"Can we just go?" Orion huffed. They could feel the watchful gazes of neighbors on their skin. "Or does treating me like a six-year-old in public help you play pretend you actually know what you're doing?"

Orion felt the air still. Not the kind of stillness that comes when you're alone with just your thoughts and the vast open world, but the stillness that comes when everyone around you holds their breath, waiting for a bomb to detonate.

Orion had gone too far. They always went too far. When would people see that *Orion* was the bomb and steer clear?

"I'll be waiting in the truck," Lewie said thickly. Lowly. "And so help me, if you don't get your ass in the passenger seat, I will drive beside you all the way home with the windows down blaring Gregorian chants."

Usually, Orion would have called Lewie's bluff. He never would've blared music so loudly Orion couldn't safely hear their surroundings.

Now, though? Lewie was pissed enough to make Orion not want to risk it.

They followed behind Lewie with one last "Congratulations" murmured to Basie. Even if Canis wasn't leading the way, Orion would've been able to follow the tangible trail of doom and gloom before them.

When they were both in the truck, Lewie didn't start it up. Orion didn't think he even stuck the keys in the ignition.

With a deep sigh, Orion closed their eyes and began to speak.

"I'm eighteen," Orion stated evenly. "If I want to take one afternoon to come and support Basie, then legally, I'm allowed. I'm not behind on my schoolwork. I'm in the top ten percent of my class. I don't take sick days. And I'm really, *really* tired of you treating me like I'm still some helpless kid. On paper, I'm a gold star."

"On paper, sure," Lewie agreed bitterly. "Do you know how long I waited for you at school today? First, all the buses left, then the other parents, until it was just me sitting out in front of the school, waiting for you to come out. Finally, I went inside, and the secretary told me you'd signed yourself out hours ago. It is—" Lewie's voice broke, though not from tears. From *strain.* "It is infuriating to not know where you are."

"Why do you need to know in the first place? You're not my legal guardian anymore."

"Some things don't have anything to do with the law, Ri. They have to do with *family,*" Lewie retorted loudly. "When I was going through shit in high school, I still had the decency to tell Eury when I would be home for dinner. There was no law that forced her to care. I was eighteen and she was our stepmom. And yeah, things weren't always simple, but she loved me enough to want me to be safe and I loved her enough to let her know I was. For you to not tell me makes me wonder if *you* don't care about me—"

"Of *course* I fucking care. You're my brother. I've got no choice but to—"

"*Or,* you're hiding something from me."

Orion's lips fell shut.

They sat impossibly still. They'd been so consumed with wanting Lewie to change his opinion of them, that they forgot the whole reason they allowed the misunderstanding to exist in the first place. It protected them from Lewie's questions, from explanations Orion still hadn't figured out how to give.

"So you are hiding something from me."

"No," Orion protested lamely. "You're making a big deal out of nothing."

"It's not nothing! You're distant, Ri. You go out wandering around town, sometimes after dark. When I ask when you'll be home, you brush me off—or worse, you lie. If you want me to stop worrying, if you *really* want me to trust you, then you need to tell me why."

Because I'm looking for something.

No. They couldn't say that. They were supposed to know where everything was. Admitting to Lewie that they couldn't find it would be admitting that something was terribly wrong with their family's magic. Orion just needed more time—whether it was to figure out a way to fix the magic or to find what they were looking for without magic. But they couldn't let Lewie get involved.

"Are you…in trouble? In danger?" Lewie pressed when Orion hadn't answered.

"No," Orion answered immediately. *I'm not the one who's in danger.* "I have a lot to think about. Walking helps. I only started doing it because that's what Basie does when he needs to think."

"I thought we raised you better than to use Basie as a role

model." Lewie sighed. It sounded like he was hoping the short stream of air he drew in would undo all of the too-tight screws in his head—allow him to think without threat of migraine or complete system meltdown.

"Talking it over with someone else might help too," suggested Lewie once he regained his cool.

Orion grimaced. "I doubt that."

"I think you'd be surprised. What about a therapist? Basie started seeing someone after he got back from seeing his mom's grave in Canada and he says it's been great." The idea of Basie horizontal on a shrink's couch was entertaining for the half-second Orion spared to think about it. But for some reason, when they imagined the cushions behind their own back, their skin began to crawl. And still, Lewie continued to speak. Their insides were a crystal sheet of thin ice, and every word Lewie spoke was another footstep toward the fragile center. "It'd be private, you know. Licensed counselors have to stick to HIPAA, so I wouldn't know anything, unless you wanted them to tell me. We've just been through a lot these past years and I wouldn't judge you if you wanted to—"

By the time Orion knew it was going to happen, it was too late. One heavy footstep too many and everything shattered.

"Don't you ever shut the *fuck* up?" Orion cried, slamming their hands so hard on the dashboard, the glove compartment fell into their lap. "If this was something you could help with, don't you think I would've said something by now? I swear, you see any problem ever and put on your dumb superhero cape and tights and try to play Superman. You'd go back and try to end wars if you could. But the truth is, you're just some guy from

Pennsylvania and, contrary to popular belief, you don't have all the answers. So quit trying to fix me!"

By the time the sound of Orion's voice dissipated, the truck seemed deathly quiet. It made the cabin shrink and their palms feel clammy. Orion wiped their palms on their jeans, every second of quiet making their heart gain speed. Why were they always so *terrible?*

Eventually, there was a crinkle of leather as Lewie adjusted in his chair.

"Message received," he said, and it was so quiet, Orion thought they imagined it.

It was the hurt in his voice that made Orion dig their fingernail into the seam of their jeans and muster up enough strength to murmur just as quietly, "I'm not doing anything bad or unsafe."

The middle seat dipped; a hand placed close to Orion's thigh without actually touching them.

"I know. But whatever it is, it makes you angry."

Because it terrifies me.

"If you want to get rid of everything that makes me angry, you'll have to burn down the whole world."

Lewie gave a thoughtful hum, as if he were imagining the same thing Orion was—smoldering ash on the ground and the thick, choking smoke billowing up from it. Choking him. Filling a world with nothing in it.

"I think the nothingness would make you angry too."

Orion gave a frustrated laugh. That was true enough.

"Then maybe the thing you should burn down is me."

"I hate to tell you, Ri," began Lewie, revving the truck to life. "But keep up this angsty loner shit, and you might burn yourself down first."

Orion leaned their head against the headrest and let their eyes fall closed. The relief on their sensitive eyes was immediate.

It wouldn't be so bad to burn, they thought. Maybe heaven looked like Long Lily.

T HE NIGHT IT HAPPENED, Basie woke to the sound of the world ending.

Except, it wasn't the end of the world. It was just his phone announcing an incoming call from Lewie. Although, at this hour, a call from Lewie usually came with news that someone was having the worst night of their life and it was time to gear up to go help. It only *sounded* like the apocalypse because Basie had changed his ringer to the same horrible blaring that Kit used on his own phone when he became a firefighter.

A year ago, Kit would've been the first to stir awake, but Basie had been a firefighter for months now. Every one of his nerves was trained to *go*. He snatched the phone from the table, screen bright enough to illuminate the whole room. Lewie hardly let him mumble *Hello?* before he started rambling off information like he was a dispatcher.

"Building fire at Loose Change Consignment located on 75 Elmer Ave," Lewie relayed.

"Shit," Basie swore.

He threw himself out of bed, his phone almost slipping from between his shoulder and his ear as he scrambled into his pant legs.

Loose Change was Frida Dixon's place. Frida Dixon, the kind

woman who kept Tootsie Rolls in her pockets to give the kids who rode their bikes past her shop. Who raised her niece while her sister was serving overseas. Who always made sure Basie was eating enough, then offered to feed him a little more.

"We're going to need all hands on deck," Lewie continued.

"Shit, man," Basie said. "How long until dispatch sends the call?"

"Your guess is as good as mine. We might be the ones to *make* the call once we get there. And don't ask me how I know about the fire."

"Do I ever?" Basie snapped.

Ignoring this, Lewie went on. "Can Kit watch the kids? They're all asleep, but I don't know how long I'm going to be gone and I don't want to leave if Orion is just going to—"

"I'll watch the kids," grumbled Kit, from the side of the bed, voice still thick and raspy with sleep. He was always eavesdropping on Basie's calls—but then, maybe Basie should've turned his volume down.

"I'll drop him off," Basie confirmed. Kit could've driven himself, but Basie's truck was in the shop and Jed was taking an Elliot century to get the work done. Basie would have to roll up to the firehouse in his husband's old van—but honestly, he was fine with whatever got him there the quickest.

"Take care, Lew," finished Basie, even though he'd see his best friend in just a few minutes.

The line went dead a second later, code for *Quit your misty-eyin' and get your ass in gear.* Basie stuffed his phone in his back pocket.

"Anyone we know?" Kit asked, stretching his neck.

"It's *always* someone we know," Basie replied, tying his boots. That was the nature of being the only fire department in a small town. "Frida Dixon's place is on fire. Land sakes, I told her to update her electrical years ago."

"Come on, Bas. You don't know that's what happened."

A click sounded, then a low, glowing lamp light filled the room. Even though Basie hated disturbing Kit's sleep, Kit always insisted on switching the light on, just so Basie wouldn't have to stumble around in the dark. Sometimes Kit could fall back asleep before Basie even left the house. Tonight, though, they were both on duty.

Kit sat on the edge of the bed, pulling on his own shoes. In lighter circumstances, the loafer-pajama combo would've made Basie smile.

"Lewie appreciates this, you know," Basie said. "He doesn't trust just anyone with those kids."

"'Course I know," Kit replied, easily. "I'm happy to do it. And you don't have to drop me off."

"No, honey, I'll take you. You're not walking out in the dark. Good to go?"

Kit answered by rising to his feet.

Basie looked him over, holding back a sigh. He hadn't anticipated just how much his new job would bleed over from his life onto his husband's. When he first started taking calls, it was easy to give into naivety that he could keep them separate. But it was their shared bed he left at the wee hours of the morning. It was his century-old lover with the bags underneath his eyes and a refusal to complain.

Basie stepped forward and kissed him softly. Just once.

"I'm glad I get to go through this life with you," he said, because it was what he felt.

They left before Kit could do what he always did and outdo Basie's sweetness with something cheesy and loving of his own. But that was okay. Basie would come home later and they could pick up right where they left off.

I T REMINDED KIT OF being in Baltimore—this moment of silence, sitting completely still in the darkness of the Simon household. It was the same feeling of being watched by walls that were not entirely his own, listening to a silence that only existed in these early hours of the morning. At first, he'd been able to hear the sirens coming from the fire station, but even those had dispersed like nighttime fog. He missed the familiar sounds of Wellhead. The crickets. The creek. This was a silence that could only be filled with unadulterated dread. Kit was up to his neck in it.

He tightened his jaw, drawing an unsteady breath in through his nose before letting it slip from his lips.

Basie was going to be fine. It only seemed worse than normal because Kit was someplace that wasn't his own house. Things were always uncomfortable when they went against the script of normalcy. Still, Kit couldn't help but wish he was still in his own bed, Basie's familiar warmth beside him. It made him feel awful to wish for something so selfish when Frida Dixon's livelihood was currently up in flames. But, in Lewie's creaky armchair, Kit closed his eyes and imagined it was so.

He must've dozed, only for a minute, because soon, the sound of light footsteps jolted Kit to awareness. The corner of his mouth felt damp and his jaw hurt from clenching it. He squinted into the darkness, recognizing Tallie by her bouncing leg and her nighttime ponytail.

"Tallie, sweetheart, what's the matter?" Kit asked. He left the lamp beside him unlit, hoping that the blue nighttime would lull her back to sleepiness.

"You were feeling too much," she stated, like that was a normal thing to say. Kit was careful not to react. Tallie scrubbed her eyes with her knuckles. "Where's Lewie?"

"He's out with Uncle Basie on a call."

"They must be feeling too much too. Can't sleep."

Kit wanted to ask what on earth she was talking about. The time and place for him to learn the truth of the Simon Knowing was approaching, he could sense that much. It made his curiosity almost unbearable.

But now was not the time for revelations, so Kit kept his mouth shut. He merely crossed the room, knelt down, and gave Tallie a tight squeeze. She did not seem to know what to do with this, but eventually let her tiny arms stretch around his shoulders.

"I'm sorry about that. It seems I always feel too much," Kit whispered. "I'll do a better job keeping my thoughts to myself if you want to try going back to bed? I can tuck you in."

He wasn't sure if what he'd said matched up with…whatever magical or psychic thing was keeping Tallie up. His guess must've been close enough though, because Tallie nodded and folded her hand in his. She led the way up the curving stairs like she could do it in a blindfold, tiptoeing all the way to the room she shared with Eliza.

With all the respect the act was due, Kit tucked Tallie's blankets up beneath her chin and pressed a kiss to her forehead.

"Sweet dreams, honeybee." Kit said, trying to smother every bad thing he was thinking and feeling somewhere untouchable.

Tallie was asleep in seconds.

On his way out, Kit poked his head into the remaining bedrooms. Meyer and Sam snored on their respective bunks, with baby Ethan sprawled out in his new "big boy bed" close by. Orion's room was right beside it, windows wide open and Orion—

No. Wait.

Where was Orion?

Kit pushed the door wide open, flicking the light on. He half expected Orion with their sensitive eyes to shriek—*Turn that shit off, goddamn!*—but there was nothing. Kit scoured the space in a frantic circle, then combed Lewie's room, then Maria's, before practically crashing down the stairs.

The front door opened. First Kit hoped it was Orion, then the more selfish part of him hoped it was Basie. But it was neither. Flicking on the floor lamp was a girl with choppy black hair and bangs, hoisting too many bags over her shoulders.

"Well, go on," she said. "Looks like I'm just in time."

Kit blinked.

"*Maria?*" he exclaimed. "Aren't you supposed to be…enjoying senior year at college?"

"Who needs the college experience when you have siblings to watch?" At Kit's bewilderment, she tossed up a mischievous smile that was half shadow. "I knew you and Orion would both be wishing for the same thing, so I drove back."

"And what's that?" Kit asked warily.

"To see your loved ones home safe. Not hard to put together

when your husband and my brother are both firefighters. Must be one hell of an emergency," Maria replied simply. She let the bags slide off her shoulder with a sigh of relief. "I'm here now, so you can do whatever it is that you have to do."

"Orion is missing, but…it seems like you knew that already," Kit stated, feeling a bit foolish. Nothing in this blessed house ever made any sense. "You don't even seem worried about it."

"Doesn't take a genius to guess that Orion is missing. Why would I be worried about it when I know you'll track them down in no time? Seriously, what are you still doing here?"

Maria kicked off her shoes, which landed in a tangled mess of laces next to the door. She made her way up the stairs and called out, "Nice to officially meet you, by the way. Always wanted a gay uncle."

She was gone before Kit could untangle the specifics of what had just happened, but there wasn't time; not with Orion missing in the middle of the night. Kit tried to stomp the brakes on his racing thoughts, searching for any idea of where Orion might be, but came up flat. And then there was the matter of Maria appearing in the middle of the night, acting for all the world like she knew everything—where Orion was and that Kit needed to find them. She'd even acted like she knew everything would be okay, she believed Kit had it under control.

Or maybe that was just her way, easy and unbothered. She'd certainly had more faith in Kit than he had in himself to assume he already knew where to look.

Kit scratched his fingers through his hair.

What had she said again?

I knew you and Orion would both be wishing for the same thing…to see your loved ones home safe.

Kit's heart dropped.

The fire. Orion was at the fire.

K IT RAN FASTER THAN he knew how.

Obstacles tried to trip him as he went, loose branches and stones he couldn't see in the lackluster streetlight. When he'd left Wellhead, he'd forgotten to put on socks under his loafers, and now was beginning to feel the consequences. Even as his ankles and heels chafed, he sprinted, throwing himself away from safety and ever closer to the fire. As Kit hit Elmer Avenue, he coughed, smoke growing heavy in the air, nearly choking. It confirmed what he already knew: this was really happening.

Just another block. Another street corner and—

There it was, the black sky broken up by a fire so all-consuming it would've filled the devil with envy. The Loose Change Consignment was powerless to fight against it. It looked like it was weeping, a gaping door for a keening mouth and orange flames for tears—an expression of sorrow for being eaten alive. The fire chewed its hungry maw through the windows, spilling over the edges and melting the plastic siding away. There, it climbed up the very walls of the building, spilling blackness into the starry sky.

The crowd surrounding the mess was just as massive, being held at bay only by the commanding words of a few frantic police officers. On the other side of the line of badges, the firefighters fed yards of hose across the street into the house, the nozzle likely already handled by someone inside. That was the hardest part, Kit thought. Not being able to see the fire die, just having to trust that it was being smothered, bit by bit.

For a second, Kit had the unspeakable urge to move to the front of the line and look for Basie among the firefighters who were safe and sound outside the building.

But then he remembered Orion and their lack of impulse control, and began to search the masses, cursing that unbelievable miscreant who couldn't keep their damned feet still.

Spectators stood shoulder to shoulder, filling the block and making it hard for Kit to wade through them, much less find the Orion-shaped needle in the haystack. He'd hoped that because Orion was nearly as tall as their brother, it'd be easier to spot their mess of hand-chopped hair in the dark. But the streetlight stood no chance against the blinding glow of the fire, which danced and shifted, too inconsistent to see anything in.

Kit shoved his way through the crowd, scanning faces in the shadows.

"Have you seen Orion Simon?" he asked his neighbors, but the question fell on ears that could not hear anything but crackling and roaring.

Then, above the cacophony, a fractured voice.

"*Lewie!*"

There: across the mass of bodies, Orion's knitted cap of sparkling yarn caught a glint of light.

Kit pushed against the crowd, but no one would budge.

"Excuse me, I have to get through," said Kit urgently, placing his hand on a stranger's shoulder. It took two strong shoves before they stepped aside, but as Kit tried to ease forward, he found the crowd even denser.

Squaring his jaw, Kit's eyes darted around the dense space. If he didn't want to start shoving people to the ground, then the only way was around. Slipping back into the outskirts, Kit followed the traces of Orion's voice, hearing it get louder and louder as the distance closed.

"Has anyone seen my brother? God, *Lewie!* Are you there?"

Kit shielded his mouth with his arm, coughing through the smoke that blew into the streets.

"You need to *get back,* Rion," Kit heard another voice say, demanding. "Let your brother and his team do their jobs."

Kit snapped his head towards the source of the second voice, louder than Orion's. He heaved out a gasp. There was the run-away, pushing up against the edge of the barricade. Officer Ida Alvarez struggled to hold them back, trying to avoid Orion's fingers clawing at her embroidered badge.

"No! You don't understand! Something terrible is going to happen. I know it!" Orion pleaded.

Kit's heart dropped. The dread was already there, waiting, and now it filled him up.

"If you haven't noticed, something terrible has *already* happened," Alvarez said gruffly, adjusting her hold on the kid. "Don't make me cuff you, Orion."

Hearing this, Kit yanked himself out of his head and away from the awful sinking feeling. Shaking with the effort to keep his breathing under control, he came up behind Orion, wrapping his arms around their waist and tugging them back just in time to stop them from clawing Alvarez's face. A startled yelp burst out of Orion as Kit drew them away from the barricade.

"Let me go*!* You assholes! Let go of me!" Orion shrieked, kicking and writhing against Kit's grip. Kit struggled to keep his hold, grip too sweaty and shaky, but adrenaline gave him strength, an unfamiliar boost of fortitude Kit didn't know how to wield.

"I will absolutely not let go. What the *hell* is wrong with you?" Kit exclaimed, squeezing his arms tighter. The intensity of Orion's fighting drained away when they recognized Kit's voice, but they still tried to worm out of his hold. Kit let Orion free, only to snatch up their wrist in a death grip. The sudden release almost sent Orion to the ground on top of their cane, but they got their bearings quickly enough to scowl back their red-hot ire at Kit.

Kit didn't give a damn.

"Do you have any idea how worried I was? Lewie asked me to keep an eye on all of you, but when I went to your room, you *weren't there.* And on a night like this? What were you thinking?" Kit squeezed tighter. "You know what, I don't care. I don't care what you *know,* either, Orion. I'm taking you home."

"*No!*" Orion growled, trying to snatch their arm back, but Kit's hold was too strong. "Kit, you have to believe me. Something awful is going to happen and I need to warn Lewie. He needs to know."

"Maybe he already does," Kit reasoned, feeling a little hysterical himself.

"That *isn't how it works!*" Orion snapped.

Kit scanned the first responders gathered in the street a safe distance away from Loose Change. They were in a constant state of motion, yelling orders and unrolling yard after yard of hose. If something was going to happen, they'd know right? But it was too messy, all bellowed questions and commands, and Kit couldn't tell if this was how it always was at the scene of a fire, or if something about this one was worse.

Squeezing his eyes shut, Kit released Rion's wrist.

"Okay. Fine," he sighed. "Tell me. What's going to happen?"

Orion shook their head, scrubbing their face with their knuckles.

"I don't know," they admitted hopelessly.

"Then how do you know something is wrong?"

"I can't tell you!" Orion sounded exasperated. Desperate.

"Rion, if someone is in danger, I don't care how sacred your family secrets are. You need to *tell me* what you know."

Orion started pulling at their necklace, twisting the chain between their fingers, so hard that the chain had to be digging painfully at their throat. It was strange to see them wearing only one, and one that Kit recognized—a pendant with the constellation Orion, stars raised off the surface like braille. Orion smoothed their fingers anxiously over the dots, blinking away tears and smoke, their mind clearly going a million miles an hour.

Kit knew then and there that Orion wasn't going to tell him anything. Orion wasn't working up the courage to confess; they were only trying to calculate a way around their secret.

"Tell me what's happening," they said urgently. "Tell me what you see."

Gritting his teeth, Kit realized he was going to have to take all he could get from Orion. He turned his face towards the fire, where the front window of Loose Change Consignment had been blown out, replaced by a wall of flame. He didn't think he'd ever seen a fire so big or blinding before. He was close enough that opening his eyes against the smoke made his eyes hurt.

"The fire is working its way up the building," said Kit miserably. "But—but it's barely spread to the second floor."

"That's good, right? That means they're knocking it down?"

"I—I don't know. I guess. Basie doesn't usually give me too many details about his calls."

"What else? What else?" Orion pressed, grabbing at Kit, their nails digging crescent moons into Kit's bare arms.

Orion's grasp hurt, but the slight pinch grounded Kit somehow. He narrowed his eyes, moved forward to try to get a better look. Dragging Orion alongside him, he tried to find a better vantage point from around the brigade of fire trucks.

Making his way to the far end of the barricade, Kit found a quiet street corner where he could appraise the scene from the side. It was so quiet now, he could hear the rushing of his own pulse in his ears, but he still squinted into the madness and filed away the important details.

There were at least half a dozen people all wearing helmets that all matched Basie's—the numbers 756 printed in bright yellow. There were the medics waiting on standby. And there was Basie's captain, leaning into this radio barking something Kit could not hear.

"The captain's giving commands," Kit told Rion. "I can't hear what he's saying."

"Me either," murmured Rion. They turned their head so that one ear was pointed right at the group of firefighters, and squeezed their eyes as tight as they would go. Kit briefly worried that the smoke and bright light was irritating their eyes, but Orion was more likely to break Kit's hold and charge right at the fire than to ever listen to a command.

Without warning, a cheer erupted from a group of bystanders standing closest to the palisade of first responders. It quickly spread to the rest of the onlookers, a roar of applause louder than the fire itself.

Turning back to the fire, Kit saw the cause immediately.

"Oh thank God," he breathed.

Three firefighters emerged from the wreckage, their footsteps heavy. One of them carried a slumped figure—a familiar woman— in their arms. Kit allowed himself a moment of relief—all their limbs were intact, their lungs pumped air. As soon as they were a safe enough distance from harm, the firefighter laid the prone woman on the backboard that awaited her and administered an oxygen mask in one fell swoop.

"Well, what is it? Is the fire out?" Orion pressed.

Kit didn't answer at first. He couldn't, because the shortest of the firefighters was stepping right into the wash of the scene lights hanging from the firetruck. Kit gasped. There he was, right where Kit could see him, still in one beautiful piece: a little smudgy, but nonetheless unharmed.

Sweet Basie Yeats.

"The fire's not out, but Basie is," Kit gasped, his shoulders slumping, feeling like the world had just been lifted from his shoulders. "The tall one with him must be Lewie."

Kit hung his head, squeezing Orion's arm. His heart was still pounding, but he could breathe easier, now.

"Orion, they're alright. There's nothing to worry about. They got Frida out. They can start putting the fire out for real, now."

Orion was all spilling tears. They let out a sound that had broken edges, but took a deep breath, gritted their teeth, and nodded. It was the first time that Kit knew, without a doubt, that Orion and Lewie would be just fine. No matter how many bitter walls they built between them, there would always be enough love to tear them back down again. Neither would leave the other alone.

Kit laid his hand on Orion's shoulder, holding it firm. He could feel both of their bodies relaxing as the terror eased away like smoke from a flame.

The firefighters did not have time to share their relief, though. In a flurry of neon rimmed khaki, voices called for more hose, more ladder, more men. One firefighter aimed the hose nozzle towards the heart of the flames in the storefront window and let loose. The hurricane spray shattered one of the lower windows, tamping down the fire in its wake. The yelling of the crowd dulled to a hum as the firefighters gained control, but Kit's attention was elsewhere.

Because Basie was standing frightfully still, scanning the crowd. He called out to his captain but Kit couldn't discern his words.

"Speak up, Butler!" the captain yelled, attention focused on the hose currently dousing the flames.

Kit gently pulled at Orion's arm, tugging them closer to try and make out what Basie was saying.

Basie spun to his whole squad and bellowed, "I said, *where's Dixie?*"

Everything quieted: the crowd, the captain, the cops. Even

Lewie and the other firefighters seemed to falter, tossing looks over their shoulders.

"Who's Dixie?" Orion asked quietly, as if speaking too loudly would make the whole house fall down.

Love Dixon, or Dixie, as she introduced herself, was Frida's only niece. The two of them lived together above Loose Consignment while Dixie's mother served overseas as a technology specialist. Dixie's mom had offered to take her with her offering promises of Japan and South Korea, but Dixie wasn't ready for adventure, not yet. She said she wanted to finish high school first. Or, at least, that's what she told Kit earlier that summer during the afternoons they worked together at Mallory Farms.

Dixie was the best judge of strawberries that Kit knew, she sang like an angel while she worked, and apparently, she was still inside the house.

Of course, Frida had been unconscious when the firefighters rescued her, so she wouldn't have been able to warn them that they had missed somebody. It was possible that Dixie wasn't home right now, but still, she would be here—would have heard about the fire and rushed over by now. It seemed that everyone—onlookers and firefighters alike—felt the same tension that was now gripping Kit's body as they waited for something, some sign; one young girl to appear unharmed and say: *I'm alright! I'm here.*

No young girl emerged. The silence felt like a death sentence.

All at once, Basie was in motion. He seized the hose from Lewie, snatching it away before anyone could notice it was gone and sprinted full force toward the house.

"No," Kit murmured, half disbelief, stumbling forward a step.

It was back—the dread, the dread, the dread.

The remembrance of Orion's Knowing.

Their desperate tears, scrabbling at Kit's arm, unable to express what they were so afraid of.

The sickly horror that Kit hadn't been able to shake since Basie had first announced his career change months ago.

Something terrible is going to happen.

"No!" Kit cried, as loud as he could, praying that Basie could hear him. "Basie! *Basie!*"

Three seconds: that was how long Basie hesitated, how long it took him to decide. To turn, to meet Kit's eyes. To make Kit believe he might change his mind about going back in after all. To turn back and run into the house anyway.

Kit careened forward, barely stopping his knees from giving out.

"Is…Is Basie alright?" Orion asked somewhere right beside him, from a mile away.

"I don't know." Kit's throat burned. "He went back inside."

T HE FIRST TIME BASIE met Love Dixon, he was walking
to Lewie Simon's high school graduation party with his
mother. Dixie was standing on the corner of her Long Lily sub-
urban block, strumming a half-broken plastic guitar. She couldn't
have been more than six, and she'd needed her Auntie Frida's help
making her sign: a masterpiece in crayon and washable markers
that read *Free Concert: 5¢.*

When Basie walked by, Dixie had not looked up from her
music. She had her eyes closed and was singing with the type
of voice children had when you knew it was what they were
meant to do. The cup at her feet already contained a boast-worthy
number of pennies and nickels. She was singing an old folk song,
older than the people who popularized it, with words that Basie
certain she did not understand the meaning of.

*"If I had wings like Noah's doves, I'd fly up the river to the one I
love. Fare thee well, my honey, fare thee well."*

The song had carried as Basie passed by, but when he turned
around, he found his mother standing next to Dixie—singing
along. That day, Della Yeats deposited a fifty-dollar bill into the
busking cup, with which Dixie bought her very first electric
piano. She still had it, Basie knew, because whenever it seemed
like it would finally give into obsolescence and die, she brought

it to him and said, "*You can't let the poor thing die now.*"

Six-year-old Dixie still lived with her parents in Philly, and would not reside in Long Lily permanently for several years yet, but the echoing of her voice was evidence that her return was inevitable. When she did return four years later with doe-eyes and a hungry curiosity, it was as though she'd never left—as though she'd never existed anywhere else but this patch of land that was now under siege of fire and smoke.

Love Dixon had not stood on those street corners, laying out the pain of her ancestors as if it were her own, only for the town to forget about her now.

So, really, the choice to run head first back into that fire had already been made long, long ago.

You can't let the poor thing die now.

Even as he looked back over his shoulder—where he knew, somehow, that he would meet his husband's eye—there was no doubt as to what he had to do. He only wished that Kit could forgive him for it.

The suffocating heat inside the building was the fire underneath Judas' feet. It scorched hot enough that Basie could feel it through all of his gear. Even the air itself was dangerous from the water they'd sprayed earlier, now a weapon of steam and black smoke.

"I need another thirty yards on the hose," Basie called into his radio.

"No, you need to turn your ass around and get the hell out of there. That house is not stable. I repeat, that house is not stable," came the captain's reply. "Evacuate the premises *now*, Butler. That's an order."

Before Basie could bark out a reply, a large oak chest filled with glass trinkets crumpled under its own embers, crashing directly in front of Basie. Flames erupted at his feet, blazing dangerously close to where he had just stood before he'd jolted back. Basie aimed the hose and doused the worst of it, maneuvering around the mess.

He needed to get to Dixie. She'd already been in this fire for too long. Much longer, and there wasn't any guarantee…

"If she was in there, we would've found her," the captain said emphatically, his voice staticky over the radio. "We did a thorough sweep."

Basie knew that. He had fucking been there when they did it. But Basie had been in Frida's room, helping Lewie check her pulse and pull her from the burning sheets of her bed. It was the captain who had checked Dixie's room, and that was where the mistake had been made.

Because Henry St. Anna—the founder of this town and architect of this damned house—had thought it would be real amusing to build a *secret room*. Basie did not care to know what Henry St. Anna planned to *do* with a secret room, and instead, only cared about its current purpose: Dixie's studio.

She'd tried to keep it a secret, but she had needed Basie's help a few years ago running more wires and making sure she wasn't overloading the outlets. It didn't take a genius to know that it was the most sacred thing in Dixie's life, the one private place in four square miles where she could make music.

They hadn't found her because the hideout was *under the stairs,* and the squad had been stomping all over them.

"Come on, Dixie," Basie murmured, approaching the base of

the wooden steps. "I know you're in there."

He squared his feet, blasted the flames that had begun to gnaw at the stairs with the hose, and shoved at the wood of one of the steps leading upwards. The stair creaked and cracked, not meant to be disturbed from its impending decay, but pulled back a large enough opening to reveal Dixie's studio. Basie could see just enough to make two important observations: one, the fire had spread into the room, and two, Love Dixon was lying in the middle of it all, unconscious.

"*Dixie!*" he yelled, loud enough to be heard over the roaring flames. "Dixie, can you hear me?"

In the light of his headlamp, Dixie squinted her closed eyes. She opened her mouth, like she was trying to say something, but she wasn't getting enough air. Her chest rose and fell shallowly, and despite Basie's desperation to drag her into consciousness, she did not wake.

Though maybe this was for the better: the brown skin of her face and arms was marred with nasty burns. She'd need morphine the second she woke. Judging by her breathing, she may have needed a respirator, too.

None of that mattered, not until Basie got them both out of here in one piece.

Hoisting Dixie over his shoulder, Basie crouched under the doorway into the entry of the store and…right into a wall of flames. That oak tchotchke chest was a pyre now, blocking Basie's direct line of exit.

Without thinking, Basie turned back. He kicked the stairs back into their regular position and raced up to the second floor. Since Basie had gone back into the house, the squad's ability to knock the fire was delayed, allowing it to spread and consume every exit path in its wake. His best option was the guest room—the last space untouched by the flames.

Under his gear, Basie's arms had begun to burn, his own sweat turning into hot steam. It was now or never.

He rushed up to the window, pushing it up as hard as he could. But the window was jammed, or maybe was never meant to be moved in the first place, because it did not budge. Not even a little.

Snatching a potted plant from the dresser, Basie smashed through the window. He angled his body to prevent Dixie from getting caught in the spray of glass. Most of it fell to the ground below, but Basie pounded the rest away with the ceramic vase, making a big enough opening for them to fit through.

"*Hey!*" Basie called into his radio, looking over the yard. "Up here! I got her. Gonna harness her up. Hoist the ladder!"

The 756 was already in motion the second Basie appeared in the window. In the long seconds it took for the ladder to crank up to the window, he scanned the area for Kit. The crowd had grown dense since he'd seen it last—that, or he hadn't originally grasped how many people had come to spectate the tragedy. But even as he noted the faces of his neighbors and friends, he did not see Kit.

On his shoulder, Dixie stirred. Basie felt her hands tighten on his arm—weak, but awake.

Right. First things first.

Laying Dixie down on the floor, Basie got to work. He recalled everything from his training, his recent experience, but this was the first time he'd have to do it alone. First, he needed to circle

Dixie in tubular webbing, the nylon wrap that most mountain climbers used in their harnesses. Then, he needed to wrap it around her in just the right way to create a new harness, one that could clip to the carabiner and get her the hell out of trouble.

Halfway through, Dixie stirred again, shifting painfully against the hot floor.

"My computer," she rasped, almost too quiet for Basie to hear her. Basie pressed his lips together. The computer where Dixie kept all the recordings of her songs, the entire album she'd been working on for the past two years. Frida hadn't been able to stop talking about the album at the diner, about all the work Dixie had put in. About how *never to be repeated* the songs were.

"Don't worry, Dixie. We'll get you out of here," Basie said as the ladder eased into position, angled just above the window. From its top rung, a rope and a single carabiner swayed. Basie clipped it to Dixie's harness.

"*Haul!*" Basie yelled.

"Copy," Lewie confirmed over the radio.

On the ground, Lewie and the other firefighters began to tug on the rope. Basie eased Dixie up, guiding her through the opening and out into the open air. Lewie made quick work of getting her to the ground where EMS laid her on a backboard, hoisted her onto a gurney, and wheeled her out of danger.

"Lowering the ladder," the captain called over the radio. "Butler, you're next."

As the ladder lowered down to him, Basie let out a relieved laugh.

He'd done it. He'd acted like a maniac, gone against protocol and orders, but he'd fucking done it! It was all going to be alright.

But then, what was that thing people said? Famous last words?

It clicked all at once. Basie was in the guest room, which, for all it was a great exit, also hung over the worst of the fire. So, maybe he should've expected that the second his fingertips grazed that ladder, the floor beneath him would go tumbling down.

Crackling and crumbling into a pyre of hungry flames, the wooden floor gave out.

Basie went with it.

He would have the world know this, though. In the few seconds it took for him black out, he'd mustered enough strength and enough love to think of the house that knew how to miss him and the man with marigolds for hair who would sleep alone that night.

I F YOU ASKED ANYONE who was there, they would tell you Kit Elliot went mad.

They would tell you he did not blink when he shoved through the crowds, tossing people aside with strength they didn't know he possessed. They would tell you a constant cry bellowed from his mouth, like a scream of shattered glass, tormented enough to rattle the soul. Some would claim it was wordless, the rawest way terror and grief knew how to leave the body. Others would say it was just a name, over and over, garbled around the B consonant until it was a mangled mess of shouts. They would tell you it got worse when they pulled Basie's prone body from the building and carted it away on a stretcher.

Officer Ida Alvarez would tell you how she intercepted Kit, how his hands were a deathgrip as he shoved her aside and shouted, *"Get the fuck out of my way!"* She'd tell you how she'd contemplated, for an awful second, putting him in handcuffs—arresting him for grabbing her, for disobedience. But then the fire captain was rounding the truck, shouting, "Let him through! Let him through!"

Lewie wouldn't tell you a damned thing, because it wouldn't be your business, no matter how small the town was.

But Kit remembered Lewie catching him by the shoulders

before he could collapse. Lewie did his best to turn Kit's gaze to his face—all authority, as he said, "He's got a pulse. That means there's a chance."

But Kit couldn't look away from Basie, whose burned and blistered skin made Kit sick when they pulled off Basie's helmet. He stumbled in the direction of the stretcher, eyes boring down at Basie's body, hoping to find any movement of any kind. There was none. Not as the medics took Basie's vitals, not as they pulled an oxygen mask over his face.

A chance. A chance for what, Lewie?

Was this what it felt like to drown, Kit wondered. To be so full of terror that it etched into his bones, but still be unable to catch his breath? His hands dug into his chest over his heart, silently pleading for more air. For himself. For Basie.

Kit took another step, stronger, more aware. With it came a crack in his dissociation where reality had started to pour through.

Suddenly, sound and light washed over him—voices and movement and color and smoke. He was there, and this was really happening, and Basie…

"He's bottoming out," one of the medics said. "Get him on the truck. *Now!*"

"What's happening?" Kit heard himself say as three sets of hands snapped the stretcher onto the ambulance with finesse. Then, loud enough for the EMTs to hear, he called, "Tell me what's happening!"

"No, let them do their work," Lewie said, grabbing hold of Kit's wrist, but Kit yanked himself away.

"Who is this man?" one of the strangers called to Lewie.

"I'm that firefighter's *husband*," Kit bursted, pointing at the stretcher. "His name is Basie Elliot-Yeats, and I'm his husband, Christopher. Please, let me in that ambulance. I want to ride with him."

The EMT drew his lips into a thin line.

"I'm sorry, sir, but your husband isn't stable, so we can't allow passengers. You can meet us at the hospital."

"At the—"

In the ambulance, one of the machines turned red, beeping out a warning. The EMT threw Kit an apologetic look before slamming the door shut.

"*No!*" Kit cried. But even as he slammed a fist on the metal door, the ambulance was already pulling away. Kit landed on his knees on the rough pavement, gasping for breath.

"We should go," Lewie said, laying his hands on Kit's trembling shoulders. "I'll drive. My truck has emergency dash lights."

Kit peered up at Lewie with wide, wet eyes.

"Maria came, so I—because Orion was here—" His face crumpled. "Orion said something terrible would happen. I didn't believe them. But they really knew, didn't they? You Simons always fucking know."

"Come on," Lewie pressed, voice shaking. "Orion is waiting. On your feet. We can do this."

Later—after—Kit would think of his parents. His immortal parents who always fled to another pasture at so much as a bad feeling. They could never do this thing Lewie was doing—that thing where you were strong when someone you cared about couldn't be. But Lewie held him up, walked him to the car, and helped him buckle like the burden was all Kit's, even though Basie was partly his too.

That was what real family was, selfless and dependable.

Kit just hoped by the end of the night, he'd still have his.

L EWIE SIMON CALLED HIMSELF the King of Compartmental-
izing because he never ran out of compartments.

They were all different sizes, organized neatly in the closet of
his mind and heart, ready to be opened when the time was right.

For example: that morning, Lewie had come to the discovery
that Orion had slept in the woods down in Creek Valley, instead
of coming home that night and sleeping in their own bed. He
could've lost his cool, but there had been breakfast to make, kids
to get off to school, and houses to knock off the market. So
Lewie told Orion they'd talk about it later, then wrapped all his
horrible feelings of failure into a neat Tupperware and sealed it
away. He laid it on top of the box that wasn't getting any sleep,
beside the container that was filled with breathtaking loneliness,
and under the wicker basket filled with regret that he was over
thirty-years-old and couldn't remember the last time he'd done
anything for himself.

See? Compartments.

As Lewie drove Kit towards the hospital in Harrisburg that
night, he packed away the memory of Basie disappearing from
that window and placed it into a padlocked security box—because
he needed to drive and he needed to put on a good enough show
that Kit would not believe himself a widower just yet. But no one

was perfect. Lewie's hands on the wheel still shook.

Kit seemed to have returned to himself a little bit. He sat completely straight in the passenger seat, knees together with his hands folded in his lap. It was his face that gave him away though, eyes red from shedding tears but not blinking. He hadn't wiped them away either, so they had to be burning his skin and those freckles Basie never shut up about. But maybe holding himself upright was all Kit could manage. After all, Kit had containers too, but he was no Compartment King.

The red lights flashing off the back of the ambulance through the windshield were an unpleasant reminder of what was at stake, but they successfully herded the cars in front of the truck out of the way. It gave a whole new meaning to the phrase *parting the red seas.*

As another car veered into the shoulder, Kit cleared his throat.

"How did it happen?" he said quietly. "I saw it. But—specifically."

Lewie flexed his fingers and merged onto the highway.

"Dixie would've died if Basie hadn't remembered her," Lewie said thickly. "I just want to start with that, because it will all seem pointless otherwise, okay? That house fire would've taken her with it."

Then, pulling the lid of one of his boxes open, Lewie took a deep breath and told the story. About how Basie had probably known about Dixie's hiding spot because he'd been there for electrical jobs. About how the front door probably wasn't safe enough, so he'd made the flash decision to find a new exit. About how that new exit had been standing on borrowed time already.

"Basie didn't do anything wrong," Lewie said. "He went

against Captain's orders, but…Cap isn't always right. Dixie's blood would've been on all of our hands if we'd listened to him."

"If that's true," Kit began, frighteningly even, "why didn't you go in with him?"

In the backseat, Orion sucked in a breath. Lewie set his jaw. He didn't think Kit had it in him to blame anyone for what happened, but that might not stop him from trying.

"I—I don't know. I just didn't," answered Lewie.

"What about the alarms on the ambulance? Is he going to—" Kit's flashes fluttered, shedding fresh tears down over the old trails. "On the way over? Before we can get there? I should be in that goddamn ambulance."

"Man, I've heard you swear more times tonight than I have in all my time knowing you," Lewie chuckled weakly. Kit turned, the first movement in minutes, and set a terrible glare on Lewie. Lewie raised a hand in surrender. "Look, he's not out of the woods yet, but he's in good hands."

"What does that mean?" Orion asked, holding onto Lewie's headrest. "He's not out of the woods?"

Reaching behind him to nudge Orion back into their seat, Lewie sighed.

"It means that it's not uncommon for the body to struggle after sustaining a massive trauma, especially a house fire. Smoke inhalation and extreme heat increase a person's risk of cardiac arrest." Lewie laid a hand on Kit's knee. "But Basie knows what he's fighting for. He's not going to let this be the end."

"Does he have a choice?" whispered Kit.

"*Yes.* Outlook and attitude are integral at this stage. So *we* are going to have a positive outlook and attitude too, alright?" His voice cracked on the last word, so he swallowed. "God, now you got me all weepy. Knew I should've bought more tissues after Eliza got over that head cold."

Click, snap. Compartment closed again.

The hospital was only a few minutes away now.

Just drive, Lewie. Just drive.

WHEN BASIE WOKE, KIT was at his bedside, sleeping with one of Basie's bandaged hands against his cheek.

This was how Basie knew the worst was over.

The present came to him first, this singular moment. Kit's cheek was damp beneath Basie's fingers, but warm too as his slow breaths clouded over Basie's skin. There was a red rim crowning Kit's eyes and he was still wearing the clothes he'd been wearing the last Basie had seen him. Those silk-soft pajamas. Probably those dress loafers too.

That was when the past crept in—flashes of the Loose Change fire and hazy memories of Kit yelling Basie's name like it was his own last word. Basie remembered the adrenaline of falling, then the moments afterward, lying in the middle of the fire, believing so earnestly that he must be dying.

But he was wrong. He could tell by the way his body burned with bright pain at the slightest movement. The dead didn't suffer. Or, at least, he hoped they didn't. As for Basie, he was wonderfully, beautifully alive.

It was for this reason Basie brushed the backs of his finger over the familiar freckles of his husband's face and said, "Wake up, Baltimore."

It was different from all the other times Kit stirred

awake—heavy, relaxed eyelids and a tired smile. As soon as Basie had called for him, Kit was jolting up from the hospital bed, eyes wide as he whispered, "*Basie.*"

"Hi, handsome," Basie rasped. His throat felt like someone had rubbed it with sandpaper. "Am I dead, or am I just seeing angels?"

Kit's face shattered, even as he chuckled out begrudging laughter. He laid Basie's palm against his cheek, fighting and failing to keep his composure.

"You scared the life out of me," he said through the tremor in his voice. "Jesus, Basie."

"Sorry," Basie managed, using his thumb to swipe away the tears in its path. As much as he hated seeing Kit cry, he liked being the ones to dry his tears. Basie just needed to get out of the habit of being the reason for the tears in the first place. "How are you? You look like you've barely gotten any sleep."

"How am *I*? I'm not the one who took a nap in the middle of a house fire."

"Yeah, it was a little too sweltering for my taste. Would not recommend," Basie said with a small laugh, before he crumpled into chest-rattling coughs.

Basie made a valiant effort to keep the pain from showing on his face, but he could tell that Kit saw through it in an instant. He was immediately at Basie's bedside, hitting the nurse call button so hard it practically made the wall shake.

Basie tried to swallow back another cough. "I was hoping to spend a few more minutes alone with you before being subjected to poking and prodding. What hospital is this, anyway?"

"We're in Harrisburg," answered Kit, settling back into his chair, shaky.

Basie wished he had the strength to make room on the bed for Kit to lie beside him. He wanted to lay his face in the crook of Kit's neck and smell the familiar scent of his skin until he forgot what it was like to be filled with smoke. Instead, Basie reached for Kit's hand, who held it gently between them.

Kit drew a steadying breath.

"They weren't sure if they were going to have to operate on your heart. You—You coded in the ambulance. Your heart stopped. They managed to bring you back quickly, though." Kit's eyes drifted to the beeping monitor at Basie's side, as if he needed reassurance. "This hospital was more equipped to handle your case than the one closer to home."

Basie laid his head flat on his pillow.

He…he *died?* What kind of immortal man let *that* happen?

He waited a few seconds for some sort of grieving to flood over him, the sort of thing any normal person might feel after finding out they'd temporarily croaked. But nothing came. Maybe because Basie expected that he'd *know* when it was his time—or at the very least, that one of the Simons would have the decency to give him a little heads up. Even when he lay in the middle of that fire, certain that he wasn't going to wake up, he still had a sense of *This isn't right.* He supposed it was easiest to accept the danger he'd been in now that it was over. The only one who'd had to live it when it was happening was…

"Kit," said Basie seriously. "I can't believe I put you through that. You were—you were *there.*"

Kit swallowed. "I was. I watched it."

The thought of it made Basie's heart plummet. This was exactly the thing that Kit had been worried about when Basie first became a firefighter. Maybe it was Basie's fault for being arrogant, because he'd gone to work every day with the assurance that nothing terrible could ever happen to him on the job. But it had. And Kit was there to see it—to have no choice but to accept that Basie might leave.

The only thing that stopped Basie from crying all over his new bandages was the nurse coming in to check his vitals. Before she could start ticking down her list, she took one look at Basie and frowned.

"You doin' alright, sir?" she asked with a comforting smile, listening to his pulse with a stethoscope.

"I'm fine. Seeing him cry makes me cry," Basie said, smiling back and nodding over to Kit.

Satisfied with his heart's performance, she asked him how his pain level was on a scale of one to ten. Basie watched some of the tension leave Kit's shoulders when he answered two, then witnessed its return when the nurse made him give the more honest answer—six.

Throughout all of her questions, Basie kept picturing what it must've looked like, *felt* like, for Kit to watch Basie fall from that window into the mouth of that house fire. He knew he should have felt just as much fear from his own perspective, seeing as he had been the one to fall, and he was sure that would catch up to him later. But for now, he could only watch the haunted look in Kit's eyes grow as the nurse appraised all Basie's healing wounds.

When the nurse stepped out, Basie turned to Kit.

"Listen, honey—"

He wasn't sure what exactly he could say to make everything better, but he didn't get the chance. That was when Dr. Rachel

Nguyen came in.

At first glance, she was a strong-statured woman whose smile was all high cheekbones and warm eyes. She wore her long black hair in a tight bun. Basie learned later that Dr. Rachel Nguyen was the same doctor who, after making sure Basie wasn't going to die, had given twenty minutes of her valuable time to sit with Kit and talk with him.

"Don't you have much more important things to do?" he'd asked her.

"Your husband almost died. Someone needed to check up on you, too," she'd answered sensibly.

"Boy, am I glad to see you awake," Dr. Ngyuen said, perching on the baseboard at Basie's feet. "You took quite the tumble, Mr. Yeats."

Basie gave a tight smile. He was usually a little nicer to his doctors, but he was prone to crankiness when he hadn't had a chance to curl into Kit's side. He didn't want a checkup, he wanted his husband to hold him—to whisper in his ear that everything was alright now and listen when Basie whispered it back in between soft kisses. He wanted to feel it set in when they both started to believe it.

A cold stethoscope on his chest broke him out of his thoughts. Basie patiently let himself be observed and scrutinized as the doctor listened to his heart, then his lungs. She gently peeled his bandages up and kept her face frustratingly neutral.

"I'm going to ask you some questions. They might sound a little silly, but humor me here," she said. Basie nodded at her to go on. "Do you know your name?"

Basie looked at her, unimpressed.

"Yes," he stated. Wouldn't they have figured out by now if he was amnesiac?

Kit squeezed his hand, but he was smirking. That was an improvement.

"Don't be an ass," Kit murmured. "That's the doctor who saved your life."

With a little more solemnity, the aforementioned ass turned back to his doctor and replied, "Basil Elliot-Yeats."

"That's one gold star," said Dr. Nguyen. "What's your current address?"

This put a small, warm smile on his face. There'd been a few dangerous moments Basie hadn't expected to ever see his house again.

"6163 Annadale Drive, Long Lily."

"Last one. How old are you?"

Basie blinked.

He tried not to look at Kit in blind panic. He couldn't remember the last time anyone had asked him that question. Back home, no one had touched it in decades. Whatever he said now would have to match faked paperwork he hadn't seen and whatever information Kit had given them during his intake.

Already anticipating Basie's duress, Kit smiled calmly, forming a three with his hand, then a zero.

"Thirty," Basie answered, sounding very much like he didn't just cheat on his memory test. Dr. Nguyen nodded, a thoughtful expression on her face. She folded her clipboard under her arm.

"I lied, I do have one more question." She bore her eyes straight into Basie's and asked, "The nurse said your pain wasn't too bad. How are you feeling *really*?"

Basie pressed his lips together. He had a strange feeling that any answer he gave would be considered incorrect. "Better, I think. Why? Should I…not be feeling better?"

Dr. Nguyen rose back to her feet and stood straight, the way folks did whenever they delivered bad news. Basie squeezed Kit's hand tighter. Kit didn't squeeze back. He only laid his other hand over Basie's knuckles.

"To put it frankly, Basie, you should not be alive."

Basie's heart stumbled over itself. The doctor continued.

"The stress on your body combined with the amount of smoke you inhaled caused a very serious heart attack. Anyone else who sustained your injuries would not have been revivable. Yet, the EMTs were able to bring you back almost instantly. When you arrived here, we did tests on your heart to see if it was impacted."

She hesitated.

"Well, was it?" Basie pressed.

"No. In fact, if I looked at your results without knowing your case, I would have never known you had a heart attack. There was no damage, none at all." She shrugged. "Even the worst of your burns have healed more in eight hours than they should've in a week. You tell me you feel better and I believe you, because you're a walking miracle."

Basie let out a breathless chuckle. "Not walking yet."

"Oh, you will be. At this rate, the only thing keeping you down is exhaustion. You might be walking out of this hospital as soon as tomorrow. What's your secret? Strong genes?"

Basie exchanged a look with Kit, laughing awkwardly.

"Something like that."

Handing her clipboard off to a nurse, Dr. Nguyen said, "I want to keep you here for another day just to be absolutely certain that your miracle sticks. Get some more rest and we'll check you out again tomorrow morning." She began to close the door behind her, but stuck her head back in. "Oh, and Kit can stay if he wants to."

Kit smiled down at Basie. The space between Kit's brows where the stress lines had been was now smooth, restored to its natural order. Even his shoulders were lighter, relaxed enough that Basie wanted to curl into his side and go right to sleep.

"I'll stay," Kit said, but the doctor was already long gone.

Biting back the pain that flared up his arms, Basie shifted his weight on the bed, making a space for Kit to lie. It wasn't quite big enough to fit him, but that was kind of the point. Basie wanted him close, close enough that Kit's warmth could block out the cold air from the hospital air conditioning. Close enough that Basie would have no choice but to feel the sensation of skin on skin, a steady reminder that he was still alive.

Kit was wise and immortal enough to know Basie's intention without needing explanation—not that subtlety was Basie's specialty. Kit eyed the freed space warily.

"Are you sure that's really a good idea?"

"*Christopher*," Basie complained.

"I'm just saying, you're already hurt enough. What if—what if us sleeping in the same bed is the reason you can't go home tomorrow? Too many of my sharp elbows and long legs."

"I happen to like your sharp elbows and long legs. They really do it for me," teased Basie. He grabbed the air, a childish way of saying *Come hug me,* but Kit's expression remained doused in bleak apprehension. Laying his palm flat on Kit's cheek, Basie gave a smile that he hoped was as reassuring as he thought it was. "I'm alright. The doctor said I'm a miracle."

Kit's eyes fell closed.

"You shouldn't have needed a miracle," he said quietly.

"I don't know." Basie shrugged. "It seems like whoever doles out troubles gave me this one because they knew I could take it."

Basie let his hand run down the length of Kit's neck and into his shirt. "If I can take some nasty flames and a heart attack, I can handle sleeping next to my husband." Basie tugged on the shirt, just enough to send Kit dipping forward. "Come lie with me."

Kit's lips fell closed.

"Alright," he whispered.

Something in the healing parts of Basie relaxed when the stiff, hospital mattress dipped under Kit's weight. For the first time since he'd woken up, Basie felt like he could move and stretch. There was pain, sure, but it seemed so far away when Basie turned his face into Kit's hair. Kit's own muscles were stiff, as if he were unaccustomed to laying beside a Basie who'd nearly been broken, but he turned onto his side and brushed some sooty hair out of Basie's face.

"I'm safe with you," Basie murmured, turning onto his side.

Basie guided Kit's arm until he was cradling it between his ribs. He said it again—maybe for Kit, maybe for them both. Kit let out a tired sigh, and let his forehead land gently on Basie's.

They lay like that as the minutes ticked away. Basie must've dozed, because when he stirred, Kit was caressing the inside of Basie's palm, focusing all his attention on the unmarred skin and the budding calluses.

What a beautiful thing it was, Basie thought, that this man

would touch him with the same archival tenderness with which he held old books. That death had been uninterested in them both, had promised them centuries where most people only had decades.

He loved this man so much that it outweighed the welts on his skin and strain on his heart. It outweighed it all.

"I'll be an electrician again," Basie whispered. "If you want me to."

Kit's gaze snapped back up to his, surprised to find Basie awake.

"Why would I want that?" he answered just as quietly.

"Because if you were the firefighter who'd brushed shoulders with death, I'd beg you to stay home and bake for the rest of eternity."

Worrying his lip between his teeth, Kit draped Basie's arm over his waist. He grazed his fingertips lightly on Basie's skin through the opening in his gown. A shiver ran up Basie's spine at the featherlight touch.

"You know, Love Dixon woke up as soon as she got to the hospital," Kit said. "They told her she'd sing again."

Basie's throat was thick.

"That's great," he rasped, and he meant it. Down to his bones, he meant it.

"When I went to see her, she was lying in her bed all bandaged up. Before I could say anything, she took one look at me and began to cry. I almost called the nurse, thinking she was in pain or that she was too upset about all the belongings she'd lost. But then she squeezed my hand and said how thankful she was that someone had remembered her and because of that, she'd get to *live*. She said she'd get to sing again. See her mother. Take her music around the country. And then she thanked me, because she knew what it all had cost."

A tear trailed down Basie's cheek.

"I think you were right," Kit continued. "You felt called to be a firefighter because you *can* handle it. And not just because you're an eighty-year-old immortal guy with ancient faerie blood, but because you would do *anything* for the people in this town. That's more important than you know, Basie."

"But—I mean, the way you must've felt when it happened," Basie murmured. "I can't even let myself imagine what I would've done if it had been you. I would've gone crazy."

"I *did* go crazy. I assaulted a cop."

Basie laughed. The mental image of it was too preposterous—Kit reeling his fist back like some caged boxer and swinging for blood.

But wait. Kit wasn't laughing along.

"Wait, you *actually* assaulted a cop?" Basie blurted, craning his head up so quickly, he felt one of his burns hiss in disapproval.

"And swore at one." At Basie's utter shock, Kit shrugged. "She wouldn't let me through."

Letting his head fall back against the pillow, Basie let out a slow breath of air. He wanted to etch this moment into the walls of his memory, so that whenever life flurried out of his control, Basie could remember how brave Kit had been on his behalf. He wanted it right at his fingertips, ready to bolster his own bravery and remind him what this long life was all for. Almost all of it was for this man who refused to leave his side, who'd nearly gotten in trouble with the law for the first time in his century-long life just to be with Basie.

"You really love me," Basie accused softly. Playfully. "Like a lot."

Kit dropped his face into Basie's cheek, nuzzling his nose where Basie's smile was the fullest.

"Much more than just a lot. I thought you knew that," he said.

The feeling of it reminded Basie of so many moments in their own bed. If it weren't for all the bandages, and the wounds underneath, Basie would recreate those moments here in this hospital room. Skin on skin, Kit's mouth on the hollow of his throat, Basie wrapped so completely in his arms that there was no threat of escaping.

Basie ran his fingers through the strands of Kit's uncombed hair, gently easing the tangled curls apart. He drew his husband down for a kiss, but Kit was easily led. It was a small, gentle thing. Kit kept his lips closed, pointedly ignoring Basie's attempts to journey past the softness of this moment, likely for fear of Basie's wounds. But he still let his fingers press ever so slightly into the unharmed skin of Basie's waist, and that was enough.

When Kit drew back, he stayed close enough that Basie could feel his breath.

"I love you." The words spilled out easily after waiting right there on his tongue. "Much more than a lot. Thank you for not giving up on me."

Basie meant it in an infinite kind of way—appreciation that circled around on itself until it applied to every good thing Kit had ever done and every moment he'd chosen Basie over all the other things that were undoubtedly easier. It was a thank you for all that had passed. For all the days yet to come where Kit would break through barriers just to make sure Basie was still breathing.

And somehow, because he was endlessly good, Kit seemed to understand. For once, he did not worry about brushing against Basie's wounds or causing unnecessary pain. He guided Basie into the safe hold of his arms until their ribs brushed together whenever one of them took a breath.

It was nice to breathe, Basie thought. It was nice for Kit to feel him breathing too.

When they fell asleep, Basie did not dream of fires or red, burning skin like he thought he might. He did not dream at all.

Basie rose from his hospital bed the next morning without any help. He did not return to Long Lily as the object of anyone's pity or judgment. Instead, he crossed the Wellhead threshold beside the man he loved as a walking miracle.

His mother's own words came to mind when he stared out over the yard of bees and flowers. He couldn't quite remember the exact phrasing, but it was something about their land. Something about impossible things.

T WO DAYS AFTER BASIE returned home from the hospital,
Lewie had still not seen him. It did not do him any good
to imagine a world where he wasn't taking care of six children
and could be there when Basie woke up. It would do him even
worse to speculate what those joyful moments had been like. No
matter how hard he pictured it, Lewie would've never been able
to be there. Maria would've always had to leave in the morning
to get back to college. Sam would've always woken up with that
nasty fever. There would always be breakfast to make, children
to get on school buses, houses to sell.

It *was* a little frustrating that neither Basie or Kit had called to
announce they'd made it home in the first place. Even if Lewie
couldn't leave Sam alone with his runny nose and cold sweats, it
would've been nice to know that on a normal day, he could have
taken a few moments for himself and visited his best friends. A
simple, *Just so you know, I'm alive.*

But today, the weather was nice and Sam was a little better.
The kids had had an incident-free day at school, and now, they
all were sitting at the picnic table in the backyard hand stitching
fabric squares for Eliza's latest passion project: an heirloom quilt.

The afternoon had an easy breeze about it, only dampened
by the handful of times Lewie had pricked his finger on his

needle. To keep their fabric patches from getting swept into the neighbor's small vineyard, they'd found clean rocks to weigh down the small piles.

"Isn't the fireman's picnic today?" asked Tallie, pulling her own needle a little too taut. The fabric scrunched together underneath her grip.

Reaching over to smooth the square and loosen the thread, Lewie answered, "Yes, my mini calendar. I believe you may be right."

"Why didn't you go?"

"Because Sam still isn't feeling well. I didn't want to leave him alone."

"Orion can watch him," Eliza suggested sensibly.

Later, Lewie would feel a little impressed at how even he kept his face. How calm and nonplussed. Ten out of ten, Lewis. Those kids will never guess just how much you've lost the reins on your own family.

"Orion isn't home right now," he replied smoothly. "Besides, I'd much rather spend time with you all."

Eliza set down her threaded needle and frowned, unconvinced.

"Really? You would?"

Lewis paused.

Here was the problem: he had no idea. He loved his siblings and had long since begun to consider himself their parent. But if the question was what did Lewie *want,* or what did Lewie like to do, then he hadn't thought about it. That was the sort of thing he placed in a box and didn't touch. The words *Lewie Simon* had gradually become synonymous with *single father* until they'd stopped meaning anything else. The other meanings had been irrelevant for so long, Lewie could barely remember what any of them had been. Sometimes, to fall asleep, he counted them back to himself like a mantra: *I was a lacrosse player. I played the fiddle. I enjoyed cross-country road trips. I loved a woman named Caroline St. Anna. I never lived without a choice.* So if Eliza was asking him to tell the truth, if she was asking whether he *truly* preferred time here over anything else in the world, then the answer was that he didn't know anymore. Eliza wasn't the only one looking at him, now. Tallie and Meyer stared at him too, waiting for an answer. Possibly wondering why he hadn't just given the easy one already and said, *Of course I'd rather be here taking care of all of you! Why would I want to do anything else?*

Just answer, Lewie. Put your shitty, complicated feelings in a box and *answer.*

But, he didn't have to.

Because Lewie looked up, and there he was: leaning against one of the patio pillars with a wide smile and an armful of food-filled paper plates, there was Basie.

"Okay, now I couldn't quite carry enough plates from the picnic to feed all of you, but that's what I married Uncle Kit for. We brought enough food for a Simon-sized army. Who's hungry?"

Lewie blinked, clearing away the smeary tears that were threatening to spill over.

Basie had just enough time to hand off the plastic-wrapped plates to Kit before all three of the kids were yelling, "*Uncle Basie!*" and scurrying to wrap themselves around him. They latched onto his waist like a bunch of baby monkeys, squeezing anywhere they could fit.

"Hey now," Lewie called out, throat scratchy and thick. "Uncle Basie is probably still hurt, so be gentle."

"Actually," Kit cut in, "Uncle Basie is completely, miraculously healed and won't shut up about it." With unwarranted confidence, he balanced the plates in his arms all the way to the picnic table and set them down without any casualties. "We had to check him out of the hospital early because his doctors were getting a little too curious as to *how* he could already be healed."

"That's—" Lewie cleared his throat. "That's great."

Tallie tried to climb up Basie enough to hang from his bicep, but he peeled her off, too distracted to give into her monkey antics. He eyed Lewie with an expression that was edged with shame, looking as though he wanted to approach, but wasn't sure how.

"Sorry I didn't come by sooner. I've been sleeping nonstop since I got home," he explained. "And, uh, sorry. You know, about the other thing."

Lewie could hear the true meaning—*About the "almost dying" thing.* Or, more accurately, *About the "literally dying but then having an Easter Sunday Back from the Dead moment" thing.*

Basie smiled, a sheepish little thing. "But I really am better. You can look at my arms and every—"

Lewie was across the yard in an instant, clutching Basie to his chest so fiercely his arms began to shake. Basie's own hands were squeezing into Lewie's shoulders, tightly enough that Basie's pulse was faintly detectable. Lewie pulled back just enough to press a kiss to Basie's cheek and look him right in the face.

"I really hate your guts, you know that? I've made myself sick worrying about you, and you've been fine for days. " Lewie laughed wetly. "You're lucky your husband texted me to tell me you'd been through the worst of it, or else I would've shown up on your doorstep myself. If I'd known you were going to magic your way out of the hospital, it would've saved me a lot of trouble."

"You're telling me," grumbled Kit, but he was smiling.

Basie backed away from Lewie just enough to raise his hands in surrender.

"I really have been napping—practically *dead to this world* for…" Basie was smirking, but Lewie leveled a glare at him, and he snapped his mouth shut. "Yeah, too soon. Needless to say, I'd still have been sleeping now if it wasn't for that picnic. Captain wanted me to come and make a speech about sacrifice and valor. I'm not great at public speaking, so it was more like two sentences."

"One and a half, tops," Kit clarified. "It was brief, but beautiful."

Basie rolled his eyes affectionately. "We didn't stay long. I was surprised you weren't there," he said.

Lewie told his side of the story. About how he'd gotten back on the night of the fire to Sam waking him up at 6 a.m. saying his *throat* was on fire. About how he'd been playing nurse for the past forty-eight hours. About how now they were helping Eliza with her heirloom quilt, and apparently everything was okay.

"I was wondering what all of this was," Basie said, gesturing at the display around them. "Is it a project for school, Lizzie?"

"It's a project for posterity," responded Eliza sagely. "I like to add new blocks whenever something good or momentous happens."

"That's a lot of blocks," Kit noted, nodding down at the assortment of fabric scraps and spools of thread.

Eliza shrugged. "It was a good summer. I've also got some catching up to do."

She carded through some of the squares she'd already finished. In Lewie's unprofessional opinion, she'd improved at keeping her stitches even and matching fabric colors. He'd been nervous that the end result of the quilt wouldn't be hearty enough to last generations, but it was looking a little more promising these days.

"I've been working on patches to symbolize events that have already happened, so there are some for you guys," continued Eliza to her uncles.

She pulled one from the pile. It was a traditional quilt block with bright red and orange.

"This is the one for Uncle Kit moving to Long Lily."

Kit's face flushed and he looked appropriately touched. Eliza grabbed for another square. This one was white with a sunflower of golden diamonds in the middle. "This one is for when Uncle Basie and Uncle Kit got married. I like this one."

Basie leaned over and pressed a kiss to the top of her head.

"Me too, kiddo. It's beautiful," he said.

Eliza shrugged him off, but she was grinning.

"The best one is the one Lewie is working on. I wanted it to turn out good."

All faces turned to him, so Lewie laid his square where everyone could see. He really was quite pleased with it, for a man whose only sewing skills came from hemming pants and stitching wounds. On the patch, two rough pieces of a large anatomically correct heart were comically sewn together. He'd even stitched the words *Welcome Home* at the bottom in bright green embroidery floss.

"I started it when you texted to say Basie would be alright," Lewie explained to Kit. He dropped his gaze when he found the Elliot-Yeatses practically glowing at him. "Needed something to keep myself busy while I was up with Sam."

Lewie pushed the little patch over to Basie, a silent invitation to look at it more closely. Hold it in his hands and feel the uneven stitches and cotton fabric. Recognition bloomed across Basie's face as he smoothed his fingers across the surface.

"It's for me," Basie marveled. "Because I came back. But this is your family quilt, Lew. You really want so much of…well, Elliot-Yeats mixed in?"

"Of course, Bas. You're family. You both are," said Lewie, looking between them.

Of the two of them, Basie seemed the most surprised. But how could that be? If the Simon family was one king-sized quilt, made of eight different types of fabric, and stitched together with eight different sets of hands, then Basie was a spool of thread stitched all the way through. He held the sheared fabric in place when parents died and lives were upended and oldest sons were forced to come home and play house. It would've been easy for Basie to leave Lewie to his business when he married Kit and started a family of his own—but he hadn't left. He wove Kit right in, as if he'd belonged there all along.

It occurred to Lewie, then, that his life was a fucking beautiful quilt. It might not have been the one he had planned for or the one he'd given his youth in pursuit of, but that didn't mean he didn't like the sight of it. Sitting at this picnic table, looking over the faces of the children he poured his soul into raising and the friends who held him up, Lewie decided it was all a beautiful quilt indeed.

"Your happy moments are our moments too," he concluded finally.

Basie sniffled, tapping the heart patch, before handing it back to Lewie.

"What can I say, man? It's an honor to be part of your heirloom quilt."

A grin bloomed over Lewie's face. It felt so good to let it wash over his cheeks and down the rest of his whole being.

Every now and again, he really did believe that everything would work out.

They sat at the table until the sun began to turn in for the night. Lewie hadn't realized how much time they'd let slip away, until he noticed his plate from the picnic had gone cold. Telling the kids to warm their own plates in the microwave and wash their hands for dinner was practically nature.

It was only when the kids were all inside that Lewie rose to clean the table, but Kit lightly grabbed Lewie's wrist, silently insisting that he stay. Basie remained resolutely in his seat. The easy smile he wore moments ago was missing entirely.

"Oh God, is this the part where you tell me you *actually* died and you're just a ghost here to say goodbye one last time?"

"Yes," deadpanned Basie. "You were my unfinished business."

Lewie tossed his hands defensively. "Well! You know, weirder things have happened in this town!"

"You're definitely watching too many movies with those kids,"

Basie pointed out. "But, uh, this is about something different. Obviously. We just have something to tell you."

Lewie looked back and forth between his friends, and the looks on both of their faces warned him that whatever came next might not earn a patch on the quilt. He stopped swiping snack crumbs into the grass and stood upright.

"Alright then," he said cautiously, placing his hands on his hips. "I'm all ears."

Basie rubbed his hand over the place his IV had been in his elbow not forty-eight hours earlier.

"It's a good thing you weren't at that picnic," he confessed.

"Why do you say that?"

Basie looked to Kit for support. Lewie felt his stomach drop a little bit. Basie only let Kit speak for him when there was something delicate to say because Kit was one who could be delicate with his words. Kit folded his hands across the table, another piece of damning evidence that this wouldn't be good.

"As you might guess, the Dixon fire was a popular conversation topic," he explained gently.

"Spit it out, Kit," Lewie stated flatly. Kit ignored him and continued just as evenly.

"The fire investigator announced that she can't say for certain what or who caused the fire. At first, she thought it was just electrical. It aligned with Basie's suspicions that there was some wiring that wasn't up to code. But then she noticed that some of the outside wires appeared to have been tampered with."

Lewie stood upright.

"That's awful. I can't believe anyone in town would do that."

"Well, that's just it," Kit said uneasily. "They think the fire might've been caused by someone they've been seeing wandering around that area late at night."

Kit let out a sigh and squeezed his eyes shut, and Lewie could feel his heart pounding.

"Lewie," Kit said resolutely, "They're saying Orion started that fire."

END

From the Scrapbook

1.Soldier Boy(s) by Alana Savchuk

CW: Themes of war, mentions of dementia | A Kit & Axe story

2.Old Men Don't Fuck on the Floor

CW: Mature sexual content | Takes place in Ch. 24 of Kit & Basie

3.Great Day in the Morning

A "What If" Story | What if Della was still alive when Kit moved to Long Lily?

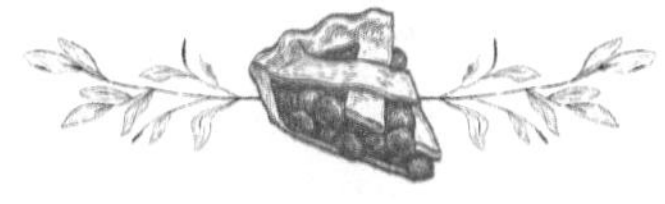

Soldier Boy(s)

BY ALANA SAVCHUK | A KIT & ALEXANDER "AXE" ARNO
PREQUEL STORY

Part I. It was a particularly brutal winter.

A T WHAT POINT DOES it become acceptable to *fully* submit to the unbearable few months between Christmas and whenever you can finally step outside without needing a coat? It is technically only a few months, but with every year he continued to roam this planet, it felt to Christopher "Kit" Elliot that *each* one of those months became multiple years unto themselves. Once the presents had been opened; once the colorful lights came down and the holiday-related distractions ceased, the memories rushed in as from behind a crumbling wall of stone patched with nothing more than pebbles and bits of concrete. Slipping out from beneath the covers every morning became a challenge, even *after* he knew he would no longer be shuffling into an empty kitchen, but a warm, well-lived space where Basie (and so his own heart) now resided. It shouldn't unnerve him, not after so many years, but he felt frustrated with himself all the same. Shouldn't he be less fragile by now? He'd seen other men with far less time on their hands move forward far more gracefully than he seemingly had. It seemed to him to be nothing less than a *miserable* failure.

Axe *had* ultimately proved Kit's anxieties to be true, and he'd told him so, having had the benefit of seeing Death appear suddenly in the corner of each room. Kit had never had such a privilege, even back then, when it seemed inevitable that they would indeed meet.

It was the last time they had seen one another, in one of his rare moments of lucidity, when Axe had managed to shift what Kit *thought* had become solid ground beneath his feet. Frozen solid, if one will. Too frozen to dig a proper foxhole with your bare hands, or even with a shovel. But there was nothing Axe loved more than earth-moving. One final time—a parting gift. Awaking as if from a dream, realizing who *exactly's* sat in front of him and *how*, and mumbling about how it all made sense now.

"What does?" Kit asked, spooning more sugar into Axe's coffee.

"How hard it was for you," he responded in a gravelly timbre, "when we got back."

"It was hard for everyone."

Axe huffed with an especially old man-like flair before sipping on what must have been sickeningly sweet coffee. ("I can't taste it otherwise," is what he'd claimed.)

"Most of us," he finally said, quiet and purposeful, more reminiscent of the man he *was*, "we have the luxury of knowing it'll be over one day."

It hadn't been immediately clear to Kit in that moment what he had meant, and he had, with some degree of shame, brushed it off as the musings of an old, dying man. Truthfully, it was quite stupid; how long it took him to put it together. He's read a *lot* of mythology. It was in many ways forced upon him. And for a while, he assumed it was something traditional and aristocratic in nature. This obsession in the West—the Gods and their moral spectrums. How important it all must be. And it was. Just not in the way a younger man imagines. They were lessons in a way that most readers could not empathize with. Morality plays for immortals because the Gods, even with all their power, often in spite of it, usually missed what might be immediately clear to those blessed with the gift of finality.

It wasn't until later, lost in the unwelcome stillness and silence of yet another winter, that he started to really consider the truth of it. Not that he could call Axe for clarity's sake—buried as he was. The impossibly welcome relief of death. Was what he had meant. The hope that one day, whether by bullet or by age, the horror of what they had seen and done, that, perhaps mercifully, all of it would be forgotten. There's that old poem about greeting Death as an old friend, and Kit, for all his remarkable geniality, had yet to even make his acquaintance—and quite possibly never would.

It was a week or so after Christmas, when the dread had *really* begun to set in, that he asked Basie a decidedly morose question. "Has there ever been a moment," he wondered, "when you thought you might die?" And perhaps, in hindsight, lying in bed alone an hour or so later, he would realize that he hadn't actually *wanted* an answer, but was given one all the same.

"That's delightful," Basie answered, looking up from his book, mildly taken aback but without a hint of dismissiveness, "No."

"That was quick."

"Well," he answered with a grin, "you'd *know* wouldn't you? If you had?"

Basie noted the obvious discomfort on Kit's face and straight-ened up in his seat. "Kit," his tone markedly less pleasant, "have *you?*"

To be fair, it was a far too long period of silence, during which Basie's heart thudded uncomfortably and he wished he'd had chamomile instead of bourbon that night.

"No," Kit choked, "I don't think so."

It was then that Basie rather stupidly realized that they had never really talked about it. Not beyond the fact of it having happened—nothing in the way of *detail* and *trauma*, and oh, *God*, how fucking *stupid* he is—

Kit interrupts what will most assuredly become a completely unproductive spiral into guilt. "It's fine," he insists. "Really."

"I'm not sure it is—"

"Drop it, Bas," he said sternly, rising steadily to his socked feet. "I'm going to bed."

A rather serious countenance had suddenly possessed the man in front of him, and Basie was reminded of the fact that an already long life *had* been lived prior to this particular moment, and perhaps there were versions of Kit Elliot that he had yet to meet. Kit in the midst of an otherwise uneventful midwinter was not the Kit of late spring, or even of early fall. Kit framed by snowfall stood straighter and spoke less—he clenched his fists more and took far longer showers than he would during warmer months. Basie didn't love this version any less, but he felt a humbling sense of disappointment at having taken so long to meet him.

✶✶✶

T HE TICKING CLOCK IN the dark hallway upstairs reminds Kit of Axe's kitchen back in Jersey. It mocked him the same way that Axe's had; the same hollow monotony following him into every room. That had been the last kitchen that Axe would ever sit in. The one he watched Bonnie cook and twirl in—the one he fed his babies in. That kitchen had remained unchanged in a way that even Kit found impressive. Especially when there had been no more Bonnie to add what were largely her own changes—fits and starts of aestheticism that Axe had never really understood but could still appreciate. The early to mid-70s had set up camp in that kitchen and never left. The pair of them had seemingly no issue with letting it linger. Even the outdated appliances had the privilege of growing old there, long past their point of usefulness.

But it was where he had looked at Axe for the last time (and the funeral didn't count). *Really* looked. Saw the deep lines in his face and the loose skin of his hands—thinner than he could ever remember them being. It had seemed strange to him, how old calluses sat on aged skin like a superfluous bit of armor. He hadn't been able to help himself from wondering if they would feel like they used to.

Kit lets the clock continue to yell at his back as he drags himself to his too-soft bed and hopes to God he's too tired to dream.

★★★

KIT HADN'T SO MUCH as twitched when Basie had finally followed him to bed the night before, and he covers him with an extra quilt when he gets up the next morning. Stepping carefully around their room, he briefly wonders which iteration of the man he loves will wake up today. He decides that no matter who it is, he'll probably want coffee and a slice of pie for breakfast, so heads downstairs before the sun's up. *If there'll be any sun*, he thinks, glancing out the upstairs window. It's still too dark to know for certain, but the moon is nowhere to be found, and he can recall something about the forecast predicting snow.

Kit jerks awake with a high-pitched ringing echoing in his ears. He feels surprisingly warmer than usual, and notes the second blanket that Basie had evidently left behind. Through the sheer, gauzy bedroom curtains he can see fat, heavy drops of snow falling towards their empty garden beds and seriously considers staying where he is indefinitely. He rolls out of bed once he catches a whiff of fresh coffee, and grabs the extra quilt for some courage before making his way downstairs.

Basie lets him sip his coffee in silence. He doesn't mention the conversation they never really had the night before, nor does he make a point of addressing Kit's odd behavior. He is, of course, *desperately* curious. Who wouldn't be, after a question like that? But he figures he can be patient just this once and let Kit finish his coffee first.

Kit wonders if it wouldn't be easier to talk about Axe before everything else. A gentler start than the invasion of Poland or Pearl Harbor—even if it *is* an ex-boyfriend. *And* he hasn't been entirely truthful before now.

"I knew Axe before the war," he starts, looking down at their scuffed kitchen table. "Or I knew *of* him," he corrects, "so I was surprised when I saw him the day we left for England."

"I thought you said you met him there."

"I did, more or less," he explains, feeling his cheeks heat. "I only knew who he was, we'd never really spoken before then."

"It's okay," Basie says, offering a smile, "what else?"

***

NEW YORK, 1942

A young, thin-limbed Kit sees, "that kid Alex, ya know, from the Neighborhood," when they're both on a loud, crowded boat set for England, but he doesn't approach him. He looks different here than how he looked at the corner bodega. Larger somehow, less like a kid you've seen in the hallway at school. He watches him thrive during their miserable training exercises—running across wide open fields, exposed bits of tanned skin shimmering with sweat. Sees him on a battlefield, even, before he works up the courage to say anything. Watches him knocking out Germans with one *mean* fist to the jaw, and plugging up shrapnel wounds with that same fist moments later.

Medic is not what Kit would have immediately assumed, but it wasn't entirely without merit. Alex had often sported black eyes or split lips, and if anyone in the neighborhood had gotten a skinned knee or some other such injury, he'd suddenly be there, like he heard the fall from a mile away. The whole neighborhood had also suspected that Alex's mom, Mrs. Arno, was being hit, but no one really did anything about it.

He would apologize for it of course, years later, to him ***and*** *to her, but Axe wasn't the type to accept an apology for something he had come to believe was inevitable.*

"What would you have even done?" Axe asked with a

*laugh, "Would've **loved** to have seen your 60 pound ass*
go toe-to-toe with my dad."

Kit had decided to go to war in the months before he was scheduled (or fated, he's not sure which) to begin his (very long) life sentence. He doesn't want his parents thinking he's petrified, so he tells them he's thinking of it as an experiment and leaves it at that. A total lie, of course.

Falling in love with Alex is not entirely dissimilar from how he said he felt about going to war (a *lie*, if you'll remember). A little bit of an experiment—an opportunity. To experience love without having to endure the inevitable loss, or to catch himself a bullet before the fact of his beating heart became redundant. He wasn't sure how he felt about it yet. Immortality. But he *was* sure about love, and how much he longed to be in it. It was stupid to assume that a man referring to himself as "Axe" would hold onto this world with anything less than his teeth. "Willfully ignorant," is what Kit's mother might have said. Blinded so fiercely by his ill-advised desire to be in love that he would be able to ignore the seeming invincibility of the man at his side. Invincible and stubborn in a way any sane mortal man should not be.

Looking back, Axe had *never* been meant for a bullet. Kit was not *nearly* that lucky.

***

According to Kit, he's Alexander or Alex *before* the war. He's not "Axe" until after. Alexander Arno was a stocky Jewish kid from New Jersey. He grew up weaving in and around early morning street markets for his mother and taking long walks to the shoreline to get away from her. He loved *her* dearly—his dad not so much. From a very young age he became enamored with the adrenaline rush that so often accompanied unexpected bursts of violence. His mother was not so much a fan of this seemingly innate interest. But she knew there wasn't much she could do to stop him, so she always made sure to have ice on hand and "boys will be boys," platitudes at the ready. It comforted her to know that the boy's tendency towards violence was unlike his father's in the sense that he never hit someone who didn't deserve it, and Mrs. Arno was nothing if not *steadfast* in her faith in her son's moral character.

Axe didn't go to war as an experiment. Axe went to war because he could and because he should. He voluntarily experienced some of the worst humanity had to offer because if he didn't, who would? It was hard for Kit not to feel inadequate next to someone like an Axe. Imagine going to war without the comfort of knowing you're never going to die.

Part II. It's not "nothing" out here.

They share a foxhole for the first time in the middle of a painfully cold, snow-quiet wood. This forest is old in a way that Kit *knows*, but he tries to ignore the uncanny feeling of being watched by anything other than hundreds of bloodshot, human eyes. It's largely silent apart from the occasional murmur of voices and the constant sniffling. It's usually deadly quiet until it's not, and there's the unmistakable whistle of falling artillery before the world explodes into sharp bits of bark and ice. The frequency with which Kit's world ends would be alarming if it didn't become so rote, and it's frightening, how quickly people are able to acclimate in even the most alien of circumstances.

Axe prescribes Kit Vaseline for his cracked hands. This kid had seemed to Axe as a sapling growing from the earth in the *exact* wrong spot. Too much blood in the soil for a root of his type. Not nearly enough sunlight, and what little rain they saw smelled of gunpowder. The fields of England, the cobblestone streets of Germany—*this* was not where Kit would flourish. It was apparent almost embarrassingly quickly.

You're too green for this, is what he *wants* to say. Too green and too delicate. "You can't carry a gun like that," is what he says instead.

"Like what?"

"Like you're afraid of it," Axe explains, sharpening his bayonet. "It'll know. Not to mention the Germans. They'll probably know too."

"So? We all are."

"Speak for yourself, *kitty-cat*."

Kit flushes impossibly redder despite the dangerously low temperatures. "Where the hell did you hear that?"

"I couldn't *possibly* know what you mean, Red."

"My name is Kit."

"Not according to Susan Greenblatt."

"Susan Greenblatt doesn't know how to keep her mouth shut."

It was an uncharacteristically harsh thing to say, especially of someone he *did* consider to be a friend, but it's hard not to be harsh here. Everything else is.

"Ouch," Axe chuckles, lighting what looks to be a half-smoked cigarette. "And she told me to *look out* for you. Poor Susan."

Kit sighs, annoyed with his overpowering and ceaseless sense of guilt. "She's lovely," he admits, trying and failing to feel the heat from Axe's lit match. "I just wish she hadn't told you *that*."

"I wouldn't worry about it," he says, distractedly watching the horizon. "There are worse things."

Kit isn't able to ask what "things" he might be referring to before the next barrage starts.

It's like nothing he could have ever imagined, even if he had wanted to. He'll try to describe it after the fact, but his words will always fall short of what he actually wants to convey. And the list of people who he will even *consider* sharing those poor excuses for words *with* runs even shorter indeed. How could you possibly understand unless you'd been there, and if he becomes a killer, what then? Who wants to know *that*?

Kit imagines he'll never be able to walk through the woods again, and the thought fills him with a sense of grief unlike anything he's felt before. He's staring up into the snow-covered canopy, trying to ignore the soft, partially muffled sounds of weeping from another foxhole, and feels his grief evolve into terror. How does one even *begin* to endure forever without the comfort of a walk in the forest? Axe tumbles back beside him before he can sink even deeper into despair, and he's grateful for the sight of his red, muddied hands and pink nose.

Kit asks a muffled question from behind his scarf. "How's everyone doing out there?"

Axe manages to spare him a look that says, "How do *you* think they're doing," before digging around in his pack for what Kit assumes will be his flask. He's not certain how he manages to keep getting it refilled, but he hasn't seemed to have run out yet. He offers Kit a sip, as he always does, and Kit declines, as *he* always does.

"How're your hands?"

"They're fine," Kit replies, pulling down the sleeves of his jacket. "Thanks."

"I know it seems like nothing, but—"

"*I know,*" he interrupts before the lecture, "it's 'not nothing out here,' but I'm good, okay?"

Axe lifts his hands in surrender, "Hey now, I'm just doin' my job."

"Yeah," Kit swallows. "I know. Sorry."

The nearest village is closer than Kit will be able to fathom, but for the few weeks they sit in those foxholes, intermittently firing their guns and dodging grenades, he's *certain* they are hundreds of thousands of miles away from civilization. He'll learn later that he and Axe were some of the luckier ones, which is saying something, considering how awful of a time it is. Not that it was going to be anything other than awful, it's just… hard to predict how very bad it'll be when you have nothing to compare it to. Axe seems far less unprepared than Kit feels, and that's when he remembers the rumors and the way he'd seen him go after some of the other kids in the neighborhood.

"Do you like it here?"

It could easily be considered an offensive question, and the words had left his lips before he'd even had enough time to process the mere *thought* of them. But he smiles, and even in the dark and the cold, it is *dashing*. The words to describe Axe came *much* easier than the words to describe a war.

*"He had this… **insane** hair," he described to Basie, "like super thick, and it always smelled good, even after we'd been sitting in a dirt hole all day."*

"Oh?" Basie replied, tossing his own wavy locks, "Better than mine?"

Not better, Kit thought, just… different. They were different.

*"You're incomparable," he said, sincerely, **embarrassingly**. Both a compliment and a complete avoidance of the question, which was shameful, but human.*

"*Here* you mean?" he asks, gesturing to the notable misery that surrounded them.

That hadn't been what he'd meant, actually. "Sure."

"I dunno," he admits, burrowing deeper into his jacket as he prepares to settle in for the night, "might be better than Jersey."

It's the first time the word's been spoken aloud between them—the knowledge that they did in fact know of one another before they'd found each other in this place, and in doing so confronting the reality of Home as a place that still exists away from *here*; a place to which many of the men might hope to return—that holds the life they knew before all this, already knowing that it will *never* be like that again, and if they do make it back, what will it even look like?

He almost wants to hit him for having mentioned it. But then again, he *had* heard those same rumors that everyone else did. One of those kids with a rough home life who maybe ate a little too aggressively at lunch, or preened a bit too desperately at the mere suggestion of platonic affection.

"*Anything's* better than Jersey," Kit lies, but Axe's shoulders shrug with quiet laughter, and he thinks about the benefit of lying just a little bit more.

***

K IT fiRES HIS fiRST bullet with his eyes closed and still manages to hit a target—a man. Boy really, most of them looked like boys, even the broad-shouldered older ones. He doesn't see him fall, but he does feel Axe shove him down to the ground before berating him about firing his weapon with his goddamn eyes *shut.*

"Did I—" he swallows what feels like the largest, most suffocating wad of mucus he's ever had, "Did I hit him?" he gasps, tasting mud on his tongue and what are probably tears he hadn't felt himself shed.

"Yeah," Axe breathes into his ear, "you got him."

They crawl back to safety on their soft, vulnerable bellies, and when Axe grips his hand to lift his shaking legs to standing, he feels the static between their palms.

"No more firing with your eyes closed, kid."

"I'm pretty sure I'm older than you."

He snorts, "Alright."

One day, Kit thinks, *I'll always be older than you.*

The odds had to have been good that Kit had killed somebody. That didn't make it any less jarring to hear it from his own mouth. He had already tried to imagine how he'd react when Kit finally told him the truth about all this, and certainly he had anticipated playing it cooler than **this**—*namely, not saying nearly enough to assuage what was clearly devastation on Kit's face, and doing nothing at all in the way of a hurried reassurance that would be so obviously needed.*

"If not you," Basie tried. Stopped. "It could've just as easily been someone else."

"But it wasn't," Kit answered, "it was me."

★★★

I F HE KILLS SOMEONE again, he doesn't know for certain. He's not sure what's worse. It feels objectively better than, say, keeping count, but at the same time, it *does* feel a little like an abdication of responsibility. Not that he started this war or anything—not that any of them did. He's trying not to let himself feel angry about that just yet. He's not sure he can swallow that feeling along with everything else.

Many of them start to assume they'll never make it out, but they *do* eventually move past their blockade in the trees. Their escape is bloody, but they're relieved at the chance to sleep inside actual buildings again. It's a slow, steady hike through occupied

France, but they enter a relatively peaceful period without much conflict, and Kit starts to worry that they've all begun to imagine a version of this story where they all get out alive.

"*Never* start to think we'll make it out alive," Axe hisses as they watch the rest of their company retreat without them, "that's how shit like *this* happens."

Shit like getting trapped in enemy territory overnight, because Kit gets a little overzealous for once, and Axe runs after him to stop him from getting killed, which is very nice, but which of course isolates them from the rest of their unit. Thankfully, and *despite* Kit, they manage to find shelter in a relatively unscathed barn in an otherwise ravaged village in the French countryside that's positively swarming with German infantry.

A few tense hours later, Axe is mumbling something or other about bread and Kit is doing everything in his power to ignore the fact that this is all his fault.

"Would you *shut up?*" Kit scolds quietly, eyeballs jockeying nervously towards the slim gap in the barn doors. "What are you even saying?"

"Relax," Axe mutters, running a hand through his unruly curls. "They don't even know we're here."

"No, not *yet* anyway. Stop talking."

If *he's* the reason Axe dies, he's not sure how he'll live with himself. And he'll have to live with it for a *long* time. He's not sure how it even happened—one moment it was him and an entire unit at his back, the next, he's being dragged into this barn behind some hay bales and everyone's speaking German.

"They'll be back tomorrow," Axe had said reassuringly, trying to staunch a minor wound on Kit's ankle. "We just have to keep outta sight till then."

Covering up the trail of blood from the dirt road into the barn had been the first priority, now it was trying not to think about how thirsty and hungry they were, about what might happen if they were discovered. So it seemed appropriate that Axe would be thinking about bread and Kit would be kvetching about his audibly *speaking* about it.

He must manage to fall asleep at some point, because he startles awake with Axe's hand clamped over his nose and mouth. There's a wide-eyed urgency on his face, and he's holding a finger to his own lips with his other hand. That's when Kit hears the whisper of hay beneath heavy boot treads, and his heart gives a sharp, painful thump. *This is it*, he manages to think, *that cosmic fork in the road they were always talking about.* Either he'd be dead shortly, or he'd wake up tomorrow and every other morning after that for an eternity thinking about this *exact* moment.

Axe frowns at him briefly, like he senses the unusual direction of his thoughts, before *winking* and vanishing from sight. Kit stares up at a small hole in the barn's tin roof and watches a small cloud pass teasingly in front of a quarter moon. All that stupid bravado that had come over him earlier? Nowhere to be found. In the dead silence where his own breaths should be are the soft, unmistakable grunts and scuffles of two men locked in violent struggle. There's a brief, nauseating *squelch*, followed shortly thereafter by another grunt and an alarming *crack* that leaves him waiting for the fevered rush of several more pairs of feet. He knows that someone is dead, he's just not sure who. He assumes if Axe is dead, then certainly, he's about to be—unless he can play dead until morning. He counts five seconds. Ten.

Braces himself against the ground and turns to face the mostly still outlines of two prone bodies.

"Axe," he whispers, still struggling to identify any notable features in the darkness. He hears a cough, followed by a pained, "Yeah," and he scrambles over the dirt and the hay and the drops of blood to Axe's side.

"You okay?" he asks, eyes widening at the sight of Axe's large hands pressed into a dark stain in his side.

"Great," he answers between his clenched teeth, "just a *minor* stabbing."

Kit gently pulls his hands away and is relieved to see that the stabbing is in fact, "minor."

"Do you have your kit?" he asks, looking around for his pack. Axe sounds like he's trying to *laugh* and Kit rolls his eyes before applying a bit more pressure to the wound than necessary.

"Shut up."

★★★

A XE KISSES HIM FOR the first time in that barn. While Kit is pretending to know fuck all about first aid—trying to ignore the blood on his hands just as much as he tries to stop thinking about how strong you have to be to break somebody's neck. And how this was *his fault*. The getting hurt and the hurting, he's no better than Axe's shitty dad. Kit's face is angled in *just* the right way, at just the right distance away from Axe's lips, as he tries and fails to keep the gauze taped over his sloppy stitching. He'd seen the swelling in Axe's bottom lip, but he can feel it now—can feel his strength as he cradles the back of Kit's neck in his hands.

It's an absolutely appalling contradiction, but it still feels like spying the moon through a crack in the ceiling when you're sure you're about to die.

Part III. Just two kids from Jersey.

NEW JERSEY, 1945

The unthinkable happens. The war, somehow, ends. The newspapers say that they "won," but Kit is struggling with the concept, all popular evidence to the contrary. It ends and the two of them are alive, and in *love*, and Kit is all at once elated and dismayed by how this could have possibly happened. He leaves Axe on the train platform and tells him he'll be in touch, but really he's not so sure he will be just yet. Because what would be the *point?*

It probably shouldn't be, but one of the first things he does is head for Susan's house. He sees her filing her nails on her front stoop and asks her what in the heck she'd been thinking, talking to Alexander Arno about *him*, of all people. And there's that knowing, *irritating* gleam in her eye, and all the fight leaves him in such a rush he thinks for sure his knees will give out and he'll collapse onto the staircase like the damsel Susan and Axe both seem to think he is.

"Well, it seems like he *did*," she chirps smartly, "so I guess it worked out alright."

"That's—"

He hates stuttering. Absolutely *hates* being unable to find the right words, and he hasn't even really acknowledged the fact that he's *home* yet. Hasn't looked around and taken note of all the familiar haunts and smells that he'd been craving for *so long*—he falls defeatedly onto the step below Susan and steals her Coke.

"Maybe a little *too* well, huh?"

"No," Kit swallows, "he did an absolutely piss-poor job of it."

"He's a good kisser, right?"

"Shut up, Susan."

Kit's pretty sure she never meant it to be an actual *thing*. It probably *was* a genuine concern for his general well being, as well as a distantly related hope that he'd be able to have a little fun in the middle of all that horror. Either way, she's totally fucked up his life regardless.

***

BECAUSE HE'S A HOPELESS romantic (an *idiot*), and because he honestly can't stand to be around anyone else after they get back, he falls into Axe's strong, warm arms and tries not to think about it. And in the end, they get five years. That's far better than Kit would've been able to imagine in the beginning. Aside from the fact that they spend a good number of those years just trying to feel human again, Kit will still be able to recall them with fondness (mostly). Particularly during those winter months. Because winters had been hard for Axe too.

But they had sat in their dark kitchen and lit candles for a few nights in a row because it was about hope, or fortitude, or something. Axe is *never* religious except for when there's candles and singing and his mother wants him to be. And it *is* beautiful—the holiness. Axe pauses after each verse, waiting for

Kit to repeat the words, and at first Axe will let the candle burn to his own fingertips before relenting to Kit's stubbornness, but at some point he forgets to be self-conscious and starts singing back.

They'll make it to spring, and Axe will claim it's because his car broke down, but Kit knows better than to believe that. Axe doesn't let things "break down." He fixes them over and over again until they can retire with dignity. That car is likely sitting pretty in some friend's garage so Axe has an excuse to ride around on a motorcycle and hope that Kit won't berate him for it. Ya see, Axe doesn't know it, but *because* Axe didn't die in battle the way Kit had imagined, Kit has now been faced with the terrible reality of loving someone whose wrinkles deepen everytime they smile. This had *not* been the thesis upon which the "going to war," bit had been predicated.

Now it seems more likely he'll have survived a global conflict only to die on some sharp-bended backroad in upstate New York, and *that* is somehow less bearable than the alternative. The foxhole option—the abandoned barn, dirty field hospital option. Despite his concern, Kit will admit that there is a certain… allure to riding with him. At being able to wrap his arms around Axe's waist without anyone wondering why. And logically, he could understand why Axe would be interested in the bike clubs. A lot of them had come back from the war without a purpose worth dying for. They came back broken and different and no one knew how to handle them, so they didn't really. Not in any way that actually mattered. It was part of the reason *why* they rode motorcycles without helmets and drank themselves to sleep.

★★★

THE YEARS PASS WITH a few more menorahs, a few more road trips, and *a lot* more baggage. They meet Bonnie Spicer about a year before it all falls apart. She's lounging in this bar that Kit is slowly starting to abhor—staring down at the jukebox with a worn paperback held open in her left hand. Axe is already several beers deep and Kit is just so relieved to see something new that he imbues the as yet unknown woman before him with all of his rapidly dwindling hope. Nat King Cole croons along to the gentle, opening strains of "Mona Lisa," and he watches her eyes shut briefly before strolling back to her corner booth.

He looks longingly (pathetically) at Axe for a brief second before resolving to speak to the person he has perhaps naively decided is going to make this day something better than what it had been when he'd been lying in bed that morning wondering why he was alone. The amber light on the wall above her halos the crown of her head in what others would call an innocuous way, but which he thinks might be prophetic. And could he really be blamed for it? He was supposed to live *forever*. What the hell's a little prophesying to *that*?

She's glaring up at him before he can speak—either because he's interrupting her reading or because he's a man approaching a woman he doesn't know in a bar at 1 in the afternoon—both easily plausible. It would seem to be a title he's never heard of (he's able to suss out *The Parasites*), which is just his luck, really. Her words sound like they're from Jersey but far away—as if she were shouting at him from the other side of the river.

"Can I help you?"

I hope so. "Sorry," is and will continue to be an appropriate first word, however unhelpful it ultimately is. "I don't usually spend time in bars while the sun's still out."

"Obviously," she says with an uncomfortable degree of familiarity before returning to her paperback, having confidently assessed that he's not a threat. Annoying, but not dangerous. He looks back to Axe again, evidently long enough that when he's turned around the woman's gaze has evolved from hostile to curious. She takes pity on him, even though he definitely doesn't deserve it. "Bonnie," she says, offering her hand.

Takes pity on them both, really, after Axe squeezes in across from him as if he'd been there the entire time, and Bonnie doesn't miss a beat. Bonnie goes to bars before 7 PM and likes to ride bikes that make Kit nervous. She also has seemingly no issue with the fact that her two male friends enjoy sleeping in the same bed, which in those days had been a pretty major prerequisite for friendship.

For a relatively short yet peaceable period of time, the three of them are like their own little family. They keep tabs on one another's whereabouts and usually share several meals together a week. Bonnie's relationship with her family had been complicated, and she frequently crashed on their couch. Occasionally, if it was cold enough, they'd make room for her in their bed, but nothing had ever happened. At least not while Kit had been there.

He would've envied Bonnie if he hadn't liked her so much. He began to find it comforting, actually, to know that Axe wouldn't be alone. Was what he told himself—to feel better about the fact that he was harboring spiteful, unkind feelings towards a woman who had done nothing other than be their (very) good friend.

It would be a shameful number of years before he could mean it without a hint of malice, before he had written her a letter he had rediscovered following her death, tucked away in the drawer of her nightstand. He suspected Axe had never known of its existence, or he certainly would've heard otherwise, and dammit, if that didn't make Kit love her all the more.

December 24, 1960

Dear ~~Bonnie~~ Mrs. Arno,

I humbly ask that you take this letter as it is intended, and worry little about its author. They are not so important. I won't belabor the point—I knew your husband, ~~Axe~~ Alexander during the war. He saved my life, and I feel obligated, particularly during this time of year, to think of him and hope he is well. It is my most fervent wish to know that he is as well looked after as he looked after ~~me~~ us.

In Gratitude,
A. Frend

It pained him all the more to know she had to have known it was from him. They'd traded enough of their own notes and letters back and forth for her to have recognized his handwriting—the infuriatingly elegant way he "spoke," even in a casual missive.

And so he began to quietly hope that his lover would fall in love with someone else, even if his own heart broke in the process.

★★★

EVENTUALLY, KIT DEVELOPS A morbidly perverse enjoyment of watching Axe sleep—as if he were microdosing on a grief he didn't even know yet. Alexander Arno without the impossibly distracting beauty of his every movement; the almost perfect stillness he was destined to attain. He says "enjoyment," really it's more accurate to say "relief," since he's spent nearly every day since they had returned home trying not to think about it. Sharing a mattress on the floor with his ruggedly handsome, alcoholic lover, seemingly unable to detach himself from what will inevitably kill some other part of his soul he'll never be able to get back.

Against his better judgment, he asks his father for advice, and when Kit's father gave advice, his accent became Irish in a way that sounded hilariously put on. "If you'll insist on going through with it," he admitted with a defeated sigh, "you'll have to dispense with that chip on your shoulder."

And he did try. He *did*. He just wasn't strong enough to bear it.

> *It's hard to confront the truth of his having given up.*
> *Because he did. Give up.*

> *"Kit," Basie starts with a dangerous softness—the kind*
> *of gentleness that will trigger tears and other unpleasant-*
> *ness. "You didn't give up—"*

"I did," he insists, ignoring Basie's attempts to place a hand on his shoulder. Gave up on the two of them, on **Axe**, on what little time they might've had left, however short—

"You weren't what he needed," Basie interrupted, with a little less tear-triggering gentleness. *"And he wasn't what you needed. Sometimes that's all it is, Kit."*

Something so simple shouldn't hurt so much, but it does. Sometimes that's all it is.

Inevitably, trying to describe Axe stops being easy and becomes more like trying to describe how it feels to see a human being dissolve into pink mist. He used to be the person that his words leaned towards, like they were drawn to his orbit. Now, it seemed as if he couldn't catch them because he was afraid of what they might say. He saw the way that Axe looked at Bonnie, and the way she tried not to look at him. He knew he was supposed to be angry about it, but there were just *so many* other things to be angry about. And when the time came, Axe, the man calling himself *Axe*? He wasn't nearly as angry as Kit seemed to be.

"It was because of you," he admitted, years later, years older—finding it hard to remember how old he was or where his wife had gone, but when Kit had sat in front of him, just as young as the day he'd left, it was like all the lights had come back on. *"I was gentler because of you."*

Their relationship had already been on its last legs when it became evident that he would have to leave. He always knew that he would have to eventually, although there would be moments in the years that followed when he wondered if he hadn't been something like a coward. Like he'd never gotten off the floor of that barn while Axe bloodied his hands for him.

As Kit began to admit to himself he was no longer aging, he was finally forced to reconcile with the fact that the only seemingly infinite thing about the man he loved was the way his body never stopped looking like it had just walked off a battlefield—or was about to walk back onto one. It had been reassuring at first, to know that he wasn't alone in his inability to manage the trauma of their shared experiences, but at some point, he started looking at Axe and all he could see was that boy in France who'd never made it home because of *him*.

***

O N A CHILLY SUMMER morning, before even the birds have begun their chirping, Kit quietly packs a bag and waits for Axe at the kitchen table with two cups of coffee. He's not quite sure how else to do this. Knows that there will never be a perfect way, but he can't imagine allowing Axe to wake up to the heaviness of an empty home. And he knows he won't be alone for long.

It feels something like divine intervention, that during their last meeting, Axe is able to remain aware long enough to take Kit's hand and let him know that it all worked out the way it was meant to. That he doesn't know how Kit's here, but he knows why he left, and that maybe, if all of this wasn't some delusion, that maybe Kit could just say Axe's name every once in a while. Bonnie's too. So the world didn't forget them.

Kit just nods, gently squeezes Axe's thin, cold hand. How could it?

Sitting on the front porch with Basie, watching the snow fall, he realizes that the bitter cold is what helps him carry the weight of it all. It holds onto it when he's not looking, and gives it back for a few months every year. It's less about trying to make himself forget, and more about letting himself grieve. Not only for himself and who he was before, but for everyone else—for the Axe he could not hold onto, and who could not hold onto him. He breathes in the cold air, relishes the smooth, unblemished skin of his hands, and smiles.

Old Men Don't Fuck on the Floor

Tess Carletta | Mature Content

Kit Elliot was an old man.

He'd always *acted* like one, but now that Basie knew how old Kit was, he could see it in everything Kit did. Everything he was. When Basie said something Kit found amusing, it was an old man's laughter that always seemed to rumble from low in Kit's chest. His smile came just as easy, like he'd worn it so many times, it was more effort to take it off than put it on. Basie was certain the century up Kit's belt was the cause of his old-fashioned ways—the very ones that stopped them from stripping each other naked on the floor of the Wellhead shed the day Basie returned from Berkeley Springs.

If it had been up to Basie, he would've undone the button of Kit's dress pants right then and there. It didn't matter to him that they were horizontal on the floor of the shed—especially because Kit had done such a nice job dressing it all up. Hell, Basie thought there might be a foam pad underneath the area rug, cushioning Kit's back after Basie had crawled into his lap.

All that mattered to Basie was that he was home. He was with Kit, who—*miraculously*—still loved him as if he'd never left. And now, he got to taste all along Kit's freckled throat until marks of rose and midnight blue blossomed all over the sweet, pale skin.

Basie couldn't remember the last time he'd done this, but his muscles did. He let his hands move on their own volition, delighting in the soft planes of Kit's chest. He grinned as they found his waist, pulling up so that they were aligned together, right where Basie's need was unendurable. They weren't nearly close enough. Basie bore his weight down, desperate to feel Kit through the thin fabric of his pants.

Kit broke away with a cracked, little moan. He combed a hand through Basie's hair, a silent message to *Wait a second.*

"Not on the floor, Bas," Kit breathed.

Basie made sure his flicker of disappointment didn't show on his face. Maybe when he was a hundred and three, Basie wouldn't want to have sex on the floor either. And if Kit wanted to wait, wanted to sort out his hurt or recover from the shock of the day, Basie didn't mind, especially now that he knew they had enough time. Maybe they didn't have forever, but they had the next best thing.

Kit's hold in Basie's hair tightened, drawing Basie's attention back to his face. "At least, not the first time," he continued.

Alright, *that* was something Basie could work with. He brushed the backs of his fingers over Kit's flushed face, urging the sweet patches of red to linger a few moments longer.

"But you want to?" Basie asked softly.

Kit's head dropped back onto the floor with a soft *thud* and Basie was glad for the rug pad. Kit swallowed, the bobbing of his Adam's apple so mesmerizing, Basie had to hold himself back from taking another taste.

"*Yes,*" Kit said like he was miserable with unsated lust. Possibly, he was a second away from taking back his word to let Basie have him right here on the floor. Only, it occurred to Basie that taking this man on the floor of this shed would be like smearing mud all over Michaelango's David. Some things had to be treated with more reverence for the beauty they possessed.

Basie kissed the patch of freckles behind Kit's ear as he continued, "I am a man of weak will when it comes to you, Basie Yeats. Stand up so I can take you to bed."

Hooooly shit. Basie thought he might've felt those words shoot straight between his legs.

He scurried back to his feet, tugging Kit along with him. Later, he wouldn't remember crossing the yard into the house, would only know he had from all the loose grass stuck to the bottoms of his bare feet.

But everything else? Basie's mind clung to the details like a vice, cataloging every breathtaking sensation so he wouldn't forget them. Not that he'd ever want to. The rush of Kit mouthing along Basie's throat was too sweet, the softness of his hair between Basie's fingers was too alluring. To give up any part of this moment would be like handing over a piece of himself.

Basie had never walked backwards up the stairs before. It would've been nice to say he was a casanova, tugging Kit after him with the grace of a lover who'd taken a dozen men to his bed before, but that would've been a lie. Basie's feet bumped into the back of each stair, making him wobble and clutch onto Kit to keep from tumbling all the way back to the bottom. He managed one even-footed step, then another, then got cocky.

Some of the stupid grass on the bottom of his feet hit the step wrong, sending Basie flying back. He landed on his ass with a yelped curse. Kit threw his head back and howled out laughter, which would have humbled Basie if it hadn't reminded Basie just how much he missed Kit's laugh. Basie craned his head up to get a closer look, only to notice he was eye-level with the bulge of Kit's pants. The laughter echoing across the stairwell died away the second Basie grabbed the soft roundness of Kit's ass. Basie pulled him in, giving Kit's cock a lengthy kiss through the fabric, before nuzzling it with the side of his face.

Kit let out a helpless sigh, hand flying to the wall to hold himself up. The desperate hand almost knocked a picture off its nail, so Kit pulled Basie up by the chin and said, "The bedroom. Now. Before we tear this house apart." He sealed the statement with a kiss that made Basie want to slide back to the ground.

Wrangling command over all of his self-control, Basie made it to his old bedroom and dove onto the bed. The mattress held him the familiar way it always did, giving Basie a strange sense of relaxation through all of his tightly wound up urgency.

Kit was close behind, crawling into the cradle of Basie's open legs. Their lips met halfway so hard Basie's teeth almost cut into Kit's mouth. The strength Kit had been using to hold steady drained away, making him drop lower to where Basie was hot and aching. If Basie didn't get Kit out of his clothes *now,* he was worried he might actually pass away.

Kit's shirt put up no fight when Basie tugged the ends free from the dress pants, but Basie found his own fingers shook when he tried to undo the buttons.

Noticing Basie's effort, Kit ground his hips down, smiling when Basie's hands flew to hold them. He unbuttoned the shirt himself, working from the top and grinding down with every button freed. Basie felt his nails pressing too deep into Kit's body, so he threw them to the sheets instead. Kit unburdened one of his hands to bring Basie's grasp back to his hip.

"I don't want to hurt you," Basie choked out.

"You aren't. I want you to mark me," Kit hummed, mouth at the open v of Basie's own shirt. He ran a featherlight touch under the hem, eliciting a star cluster of goosebumps on Basie's skin. "It'll remind me you're *here*. That you're mine."

Kit's hand slid up to the skin above Basie's heart, gently grazing his nipple.

"*Great day in the morning,*" Basie murmured.

"I missed you," Kit continued. "If I didn't know any better, I'd say you missed me."

Basie wrapped his arms around Kit, spinning them so Kit laid flat against the bed, chest heaving. Basie tugged his own shirt off by the back collar and tossed it aside. He laid his bare chest over Kit's, lingering as the sensation washed over him. At the moment, he couldn't rightly remember why he'd left Long Lily. Why he'd ever done a single thing in his life that wasn't lying his skin overtop Kit Elliot's and sharing this intoxicating heat.

Kit marveled at Basie's bare skin, lips parted. He pushed up, kissing Basie on the ascent, keeping their ribs aligned. Pleasure tore through the base of Basie's neck as Kit buried his hands in the ruffled tangle of Basie's curls.

"Tell me what you want," Basie begged against Kit's mouth. "Let me take care of you. Let me show you—" They fell into another deep kiss like forces beyond their understanding had given them a shove. Basie forced himself back, laying his forehead on Kit's. "I want you to *know*."

"I do know," Kit promised, a light smile in his voice. "I want whatever you do. As long as you're here. That's all I want."

Basie looked over the man before him, from his tousled hair to the flush rising from his beltline. The longer he stared, the more he felt his own heart climbing into his throat. It occurred to him that perhaps whatever strings of fate twisted them together had given Basie more than he deserved. It'd be a while before the guilt of his leaving wore off for good, he knew that easily. So why should this *beautiful* man sit in his lap and say he wanted whatever Basie did?

It wouldn't do. Kit needed to know he was Basie's highest priority, the object of his consuming adoration. This wouldn't be about Basie's pleasure, not if he could help it. This would be about giving Kit everything he deserved.

Basie gave Kit a gentle shove. Kit took the hint, a gleam of interest in his warm gaze, gently laying back to let Basie have his way with him. He released a long stream of breath when Basie undid his belt, chuckling low when Basie brandished it away from the belt loops and tossed it onto the floor. The pants came next, revealing evidence of an impressive length straining against Kit's briefs.

"Speak now or forever hold your peace, Baltimore," Basie said, rubbing his hands up and down Kit's thighs to keep occupied until he received his consent.

Kit lifted his head off the bed and looked down at Basie through hazy lashes, only to drop it right back.

"Oh god, do you have any idea how good you look?" he lamented. "Whatever beautiful plans your mind is brewing, I'm yours for the taking."

A sideways grin spread across Basie's face. He savored every second of pulling Kit's briefs down, unable to hold back a hot sigh when Kit was finally visible to him—the entire rosy, velvet length begging to be swallowed down. Basie craved to bring Kit over the precipice without waiting another second, but he still sat back on his haunches and looked at Kit Elliot in all his bare beauty.

"Do you have any idea how good *you* look?" Basie said. His stomach swooped as Kit bit his lip, covering his face with his hands. Basie gently nudged Kit's legs apart and laid in the welcoming cradle of Kit's thighs. "Don't be shy, baby. You're in good hands."

Kit let out a breathy, pained chuckle, only to cut off when Basie took the head of Kit's cock into his mouth and sucked. Following an instinct he didn't remember he had, one of Basie's hands came up to grasp Kit's length, stroking in time with his mouth. He fixed all his attention to the task, not daring to turn away from this vital worship of his lover's body.

Still, Basie found he was still hungry. Still curious at what else there was to discover from Kit's naked body. Basie ached to touch—and well, he *did* have one free hand. It slipped under Kit's weight and cupped the soft, plump skin of his ass. A finger dipped over the flushed curve, trailing closer to where Kit was most sensitive.

Kit's hips jolted up, either in pleasure or surprise, but Basie didn't back away. Through the garbled apology that was mostly incoherent rambling and moans, he continued his worship. When Basie spared a peek up, he found Kit's face was flushed a pretty red, lips glossy and raw.

As soon as their eyes met, Kit's hands tangled in the roots of Basie's hair, tugging him away.

"A moment, I beg you," Kit breathed.

Basie obeyed, though the swollen, red cock straining so close to his face proved tempting. In the gasping breaths he gained his composure, Kit grinned down at Basie, caressing the side of his face and combing his fingers through Basie's curls.

"I don't suppose I can convince you to lay here and let me repay the favor," he said, smile lopsided. "I'm a bit out of practice, but I hear it's like riding a bike."

Basie wanted it. He'd be silly not to when Kit's lips were so wet and kiss-swollen, and he was looking at Basie like he'd brought the entire universe into existence just by taking his clothes off.

But more than that, he wanted Kit as close as he could get him. He wanted to test the boundaries of human existence until all their real and intangible parts were a breath apart, ready to meld together. They had the rest of their immortal lives to taste and discover.

Basie climbed up Kit's body until he was laying over his freckled chest. He nearly fell off course when their hips aligned and he felt their stiff, velvet skin brush together. But he managed to press a kiss to Kit's sternum, long enough to feel the pulse racing.

"How do you like it?" Basie murmured. Before Kit could say something entirely *good* about wanting to do it the way *Basie* liked it, Basie kissed him and said, "I'm not picky. I want it however you do."

"Ordinarily, I like to give it. Be in control," Kit confessed quietly. Basie felt like a dog in heat hearing a hint of dirty talk pour out of Kit's mouth, ready to sit and heel at his lover's command. He would've laid back on the bed with his knees open, pleading for a compliment, but Kit's arms wrapped around him. Kit's lips fell on Basie's ear, sending a shiver up his spine. "But I want to be close to you. I want you to give me as much as you're able. I want to remember it."

Basie thought he understood. If he'd been the one left behind, he'd want the physical reminder too. Of how much Kit loved him. That he meant it when he said he would stay. Kit believed Basie's words of promise and apology, but it was another thing entirely to *feel* it. To be taken with so much adoration that no doubts could survive. If that's what Kit wanted—to be fucked into forgetting all the pain of their separation, to start over in this bed—that's what Basie would do.

"I've got you," promised Basie, kissing the hollow of Kit's throat. "Are you ready now, or would you feel more comfortable if you went and freshened up?"

Kit hesitated. There was probably a part of him that didn't want to move from this spot until he'd been thoroughly satisfied. But then, he was Kit *"I need everything to be neat and clean"* Elliot—and he probably hadn't been expecting to have sex today, much less be on the receiving end.

With a sigh, Kit rolled out from underneath Basie and padded away sullenly. And for all Kit was grumpy at having to press pause, Basie enjoyed the view of his perfect ass as he went.

"Don't move," said Kit from the door, and there was a hint of…something. Command. *Authority.* A hard backing to the words that could have held Basie in place for the rest of time.

He could not seem to get enough air in his lungs as he nodded obediently and said, "Wouldn't dream of it. Unless you…want company? I'd happily join you in the shower."

Basie might as well have suggested that he run naked up and down their country road for all Kit Elliot's jaw dropped.

"Absolutely not! I need—" Kit gestured vaguely, face running an entirely different shade of red. "I need *privacy*." Basie began to protest, but Kit held up a hand. "I don't care where your mouth just was. You are not going to be in the room while I…" Another vague gesture. "Freshen up."

Basie nodded with mock understanding. In a tactical move, he rolled to display the entire length of his body.

"What's the probability I can change your mind?"

Kit's eyes devoured Basie sprawled out on the bed like a man who hadn't indulged in a very, very long time. There was a short instant that Basie thought—*hoped*—his dirty tactics had worked. Another second of Kit's eyes on all of Basie's neglected inches begging to be touched, and the man's self-control would break. But Kit squeezed his eyes shut, balling his fingers into tight fists, and fled from the room. He disappeared into the hall, the words *You're a menace, Basie Yeats* trailing behind him.

There Basie was, alone with himself and a strange feeling he did not think a word existed for. The oddity of feeling like a stranger in his own bed. The disorienting sense that the last six months did not exist. That he'd never left.

Kit had been sleeping with Basie's old country quilts, giving all the familiar threaded seams his scent. Basie smothered his face into the soft fabric, inhaling the hints of apple and sumac. Basie didn't think he'd felt so weightless since before he left Long Lily. Laying naked on a bed that smelled like Kit Elliot, waiting for Kit Elliot, it was all rather nice.

The only problem was Basie was not a patient man. As the minutes ticked by, the waiting weighed down on itself, making Basie squirm. The bedside clock, one of those old double-bell numbers most people couldn't work anymore, showed only ten minutes had passed, but it might as well have been a century.

When he felt like he might actually vibrate out of his skin, Basie fussed with the necessary logistics, searching Kit's bedside table for any relevant supplies. There was an unopened box of condoms, which made the possessive part of Basie give a small smile. Next to it, there was a half-empty bottle of lube, which made Basie's smile widen, until the fantasy of Kit finding pleasure on Basie's bed made him hard and aching again.

He was willing to bet somewhere in this room, more evidence of Kit's sexuality begged to be discovered. But for today, he wanted it to be the two of them—just skin and flesh and thundering pulses.

Basie placed the lube on the bedside table, close enough to grab in a pinch.

When eventually, at long last, footsteps padded down the hallway, Basie perched gingerly on the edge of the bed. If he didn't place Kit Elliot in his lap right that second, he was sort of worried he'd actually implode.

Kit appeared in the doorway the way he usually did, as gently and quietly as the sunrise pouring into the bedroom.

Basie took one look at him and barely managed to catch a howl of laughter before it could spill over his lips. He couldn't help it. He buried his face in his hands, hiding the splitting grin on his face before Kit could mistakenly think Basie was laughing *at* him.

Except, he was, wasn't he? Maybe a little.

Because there was Kit Elliot. He practically looked the same as Basie had seen him minutes ago—completely bare and so clean, his skin glistened—only now, he was wearing a bright orange shower cap and holding two sheets of paper.

"I'm so fucking in love with you," Basie managed to say. Even though it was the most genuine thing he'd ever said, it came out high-pitched and strained, like when you try to speak through laughter but the laughter is winning. "You're the best thing to happen to me and the most beautiful man I've ever seen." Basie stretched out his arms, tears in his eyes. "Come here. Oh my god, get over here."

"I'm not sure I want to," Kit said suspiciously, though he fell in the space between Basie's legs anyway.

Through the cracks in his fingers Basie watched Kit peer down at his body. Then, because the universe loved to test the limits of Basie's self control, Kit ran a hand along the soft plumpness over his own abs, as if checking for leftover soap. His freckled fingertips brushed against the dark red hair between his legs, and Basie found he could not look away. He let his eyes drift lower—because he could. Kit had gone soft in the shower, and if Basie didn't already have plans to give Kit exactly what he wanted, he would've gone right back onto his knees.

Kit's face reddened when he noticed Basie eyeing his cock with rapt interest.

"Did I miss a spot?" he teased lowly, taking himself in hand and giving a few lazy strokes.

"Something like that," Basie replied, distracted. Lord help him, his fucking mouth was watering. *Focus, Bas,* he told himself.

"What have you got there?"

Kit held out the paper under Basie's nose.

"My last STD panel. And yours. I found it when I was going through everything."

To his credit, Basie gave the sheet the read-over it deserved. Negative results, both of them.

"We're good to go," Kit urged.

"Well…" There was still the traffic cone on Kit's head to contend with.

Basie beckoned Kit to bend lower. Kit obeyed. He let his face fall into Basie's waiting hands, eyes closing as if he were expecting a kiss. A swell of mischief itched at Basie's hands. He had this love of his right where he wanted him—relaxed, with swaths of pale skin craving to be touched—and not a damned thing in their way. No state lines. No hygienic obligation. No pretenses of *We're too old to be having our first time on the shed floor.* Just a tug of his hands and Basie would be able to taste Kit's lips and all the freckles around them.

It occurred to Basie that Kit was now looking back at him curiously.

"You're plotting," Kit observed keenly. If Basie didn't know any better, he'd say Kit sounded *delighted.* Maybe he was.

"And you're wearing your shower cap," Basie said delicately. With the same care he would've pried a stubborn bandaid, Basie slipped a finger under the shower cap and pulled it free. It rained cold drops onto Basie's face as the elastic loosened, making him wrinkle his nose.

Kit, on the other hand, was horrified.

He seized the shower cap out of Basie's hands. Like most

thieves, he was skilled in snatching and less so at the *Oh shit, I've got this contraband and now what do I do with it?* part. There passed a scary second when Basie feared Kit might bring his red face and his traffic cone cap back into the bathroom. But Kit only looked down at the damp, rumbled plastic in his hands and said, "I hate having wet hair in bed." He sounded embarrassed.

Basie suppressed a sigh. First times were always like this, weren't they? No matter how old you were or how many scratches there were on your bedpost, the beginnings were always the hardest. He suspected they could go back and forth—*Will they, won't they?*—teetering between "ready to do it" and finding some reason to stop. But maybe sex was a little like driving. His muscles would remember the hard parts for him if only he managed to get out of his own head. It might've been a little nerve-wracking to do it after so long, but if Basie had a destination in mind, the hard part was already over. He needed to put his fucking foot on the gas and let Kit sit back and enjoy the ride—as it were.

Basie peered up at Kit, who'd lost all of his steam and was now fighting to keep his apprehension off his face.

"What are you thinking?" Basie asked.

"Thinking about you," Kit answered quietly.

Basie's smile widened. "What about me?"

Kit averted his gaze, but not in the good, flirty way. Basie sat up straighter, delight dimming. For all he wanted to pry the words out of Kit, it was better to coax them out. Let them fill the silence.

"You'll think me foolish," Kit began. An objection started to tumble out of Basie's mouth, but Kit laid his fingers over his lips, silencing him. The fingers were gone before Basie could kiss them. "But there's a part of me that thinks if this doesn't go exactly right, you'll have second thoughts."

"*Kit,*" Basie admonished sweetly. "Honey, I've had second thoughts about everything else in the world. Where I wanted to live. What job I want. Who I should tell about my immortality." He kissed Kit's finger, which still laid on his cheek. "The sheer amount of *crazy* I am about you is the one thing that has stayed the same." He folded their fingers together, gaze unwavering. "That's what all this is about, isn't it? Coming in from the shed. Showering. You want everything to fit an unattainable definition of *Exactly Right.* Kit, it isn't going to be exactly right."

"Well, I know that," Kit said in the most defensive tone Basie had heard from him since their fight about the van. Still, it lacked heat. "I've had a lot of first times, Basie. That's why I said it was foolish. I know I'm not making any sense."

"Okay," replied Basie, trying to channel the same patient tone Kit usually used with him. "If I remind you that I love you more than my own life, can I offer a tiny bit of honesty?"

Kit frowned, but he didn't say no, which Basie took as a sign to keep going.

"I think you did a lot of overthinking in the shower, which would explain why you came out in your shower cap."

Kit groaned, covering his face.

"*And,*" pressed Basie, "although I'm sure the things you're worried about are real to you, they're not worth you standing in front of me—very beautiful, very naked—looking like you'd rather be anyone but yourself. We're about to consummate this fantastic thing we've got going on. We started this so I could force all the shitty anxieties out of your head." Basie grabbed Kit's thighs, gently running his hands up and down. "And based on the preview, I'd say I did a halfway decent job."

"It was better than halfway decent," Kit admitted. "If I didn't know you were immortal already, I would've known then. You only suck cock that well if you've been young and spry as long as we have."

"Imagine all the other immortal talents I have," Basie hummed. He stood up and pried Kit's fingers from around the shower cap. "If you're really uncertain about this, we'll press pause and save it for another day when you're completely ready. But I want you to know that you're safe with me. I *want* to make you feel good and—and fucking *cherished*. No matter how it goes, I won't up and leave the minute we're done. As a matter of fact, I might move all my things back into this room and take you to dinner. Then all the neighbors can dote on you and tell me *I told you so.*"

Kit fussed with his hands, before finally placing them on Basie's shoulders.

"I want to."

Basie smiled. "Good. So do I. But first things first."

With the confidence of a man who wasn't stripped completely bare, Basie crossed the room and threw the shower cap into the hall and locked the door—just in case the shower cap got any ideas about coming back.

Basie must've done something right, because when he turned back around, Kit Elliot was grinning at him with this syrupy, love-sick smile and a heat in his eyes Basie could practically feel across the room.

Rays of gilded sun fell over the quilt on the bed, warming where they would soon lay. Basie stretched out a hand, but instead of pouncing on him like Basie expected, Kit crossed the room and took Basie into a tight embrace. And, oh, Basie didn't think he'd ever been so warm in all his life.

On the skin of his bare shoulder, Basie felt like he could feel Kit down to the atoms of his cells. There was the flutter of Kit's eyelashes, the slight damp of an mouth kiss, the brush of auburn hair, all adding to a single overwhelming sensation of all his nerves being woken up.

"Can I have the reins again?"Basie whispered into Kit's neck.

Kit nodded.

They fell together like no time had passed—like there hadn't been a few blundered interludes. All at once, Kit was falling back onto the mattress and Basie was reclaiming the space on top of him. When they brushed up against each other, velvet on hard velvet, Basie drew in a deep breath through his nose. It was real this time. And there was no turning back.

It was more desperation than generosity that made Basie repeat all the things he'd done earlier—all the warm kisses to Kit's chest, all the reverent caresses. Kit cracked open, shivering with each second Basie's touch grazed down his side.

Basie let his lips follow the path of his fingers, tasting Kit's clean skin all the way to his back. Kit rolled over, unveiling the sea of stars flurrying down his shoulders. How tempting it would be for Basie to set all of his attentions to all of Kit's smooth skin. But there was something more pliable and insistent angled up to him. Basie squeezed Kit's ass, only to let go all too soon in favor of the lube waiting on the nightstand.

Spreading Kit open, Basie circled his slick finger around the flushed hole.

"Will you let me?"

Kit pressed his forehead into the blankets.

"A bit unnecessary, but go ahead."

Basie's brows furrowed, but he pressed his finger in anyway. It went in with such little resistance, Basie followed it with a second. Kit's back lifted and released as he sighed. It was the only thing that stopped Basie from pulling out his touch entirely.

"Did you prep yourself in the shower?" said Basie, affronted. "*Without me?* No wonder you were gone so long.*"

"I didn't plan to. Just got…carried away," Kit confessed. "But now you don't have to wait."

It wasn't that Basie *wanted* to wait, but he had been looking forward to finding the spot that would make Kit turn to morning mist. He wanted to watch the pleasure spread across Kit's body like a wildfire, imagine it reaching down to his toes and settling in his belly. But if Kit wanted him closer—and sooner—Basie would give him whatever he asked for.

Basie pumped his fingers a few more times until Kit's pleasure built into something workable, something that made Kit bite his knuckle and choke. Only then did Basie pull away. He placed a kiss on the base of Kit's back, drawn out and slow.

"How do you want me?" Basie asked against a patch of freck-les.

Kit rolled back over, peering up at Basie with intense eyes. The brightness only grew, building as he spread his legs and drew Basie into their soft cradle.

"Like this," Kit murmured, caressing Basie's cheeks. "Don't go far."

"Stayin' right here," Basie promised, smiling softly.

He must've stroked a bead of lube over his length, put a pillow under Kit's ass, and eased into position at some point, because when Basie looked down, all that was left to do was push forward. Both of Kit's hands disappeared from Basie's shoulders, only to reappear on his ass. They urged him forward and it was all the encouragement he needed.

The amplifying bliss of sliding deeper and deeper into Kit's welcoming warmth almost sent Basie's forehead dropping onto Kit's. But he held his weight up, gazing intently into Kit's half-lidded eyes as the feeling washed over them both. When Basie was fully seated inside, Kit dug his fingers further into Basie's ass and breathed.

Basie stayed there, still. He only needed a second. Just a second. But as moments passed, Basie didn't feel any less overwhelmed. The heady mix of adoration and reverence and pleasure and relief all swelled in his chest. And when he looked down at Kit, the sweat forming on his brow and the damp of his lips, it hit Basie hard enough that he could not breathe.

He *loved* this man. What a simple, miraculous thing it was.

A pair of lips fell on his temple, then the underside of his jaw.

"Are you alright?" Kit asked on a wispy breath.

"Fantastic," answered Basie, voice rough. "And you? Are you in any pain?"

Kit smiled like a drunk without a care in the world, and shook his head.

Basie moved. The first few thrusts were unpracticed, merely test movements for Basie's body to remember what to do. Kit didn't seem to mind. Basie almost mistook his soundlessness for a lack of pleasure, until he realized the man in his arms was beginning to unravel. It didn't take long for Basie to gain his rhythm, finding the spot that finally, *finally* made Kit cry out.

"That's it," Basie sighed. "God, you're so fucking gorgeous all flushed. Look at how well you take it. Like you were made to. Like you were always meant to be here in my bed with me."

One of Kit's hands flew to the sheet, clutching it until his knuckles whitened. Basie's own hand landed overtop, squeezing.

"When I was alone all these months, I missed you so much. I thought it would kill me." Basie knew he was babbling, but he couldn't stop. "I don't ever want to sleep without you again."

Kit grabbed Basie by the back of the neck, yanking him down so they were an inch apart. He huffed hot breath over Basie's mouth, holding his gaze like a vice grip.

"Don't go anywhere this time," he said through his teeth. The words were laced with pleasure and frustration, a messy combination Basie wasn't sure what to do with.

"I won't. I'm here with you, okay? For good. Wild horses and all that shit," he swore.

Kit let his legs fall apart further.

"*Prove it.*"

The demand went straight to Basie's core. He had no choice but to obey. In a rush, he wrapped an arm around Kit's waist, hoisting his ass into the air. The new angle was staggering, made all the more devastating by each of Basie's hard thrusts.

Kit had seemed to give up his silence altogether, now unleashing a string of curses and moans and incoherent encouragement.

"Kiss me," he begged. "Kiss me, dammit*!*"

The arm holding Kit up disappeared, letting the man drop back onto the soft mattress in time for Basie to capture his mouth in a devouring kiss. Kit gave as good as he got, tangling both arms around Basie's neck and clutching his hair. The fire of the kiss only stoked the growing heat in Basie's core. Basie's finesse of over fifty years of sexual experience unraveled with each surge of pleasure. It was only a matter of time before it came to a blinding peak.

Desperate, Basie reached out and took Kit's cock in his hands. It leaked over his grasp, a warning that Kit was no better off than Basie was. Basie stroked once, twice—

Kit seized, lips parted in a silent cry. He clutched his lover's shoulders, legs trembling around Basie's waist, urging him as far as he would go. Basie tried to draw out Kit's orgasm, fucking him through it in deep, hard thrusts. But the death grip around his own cock, paired with the sight of Kit spilling up his stomach, tore Basie's climax from him.

They laid against each other, grasping and heaving gasps of shared air. Basie would've been fine laying there against all of Kit's warmth, but it was only a matter of time before Kit got uncomfortable at the stickiness.

The air of the bedroom was cold when Basie stirred away from Kit. A pair of arms wrapped around his waist, holding him in place and combing through the hair below his navel. With herculean effort, Basie carefully ebbed away from the embrace he desperately didn't want to leave.

"Just going to get a warm cloth. I'll be back before you notice I'm gone."

A flicker of soreness passed across Kit's expression, like someone had stuck a finger into a bruise. But the crease between his brows melted into a smile, and he nodded.

Basie was gone long enough to notice the separation. The chill of Wellhead's drafty walls and windows clung to his skin. His body did not want to give up the warmth he'd so freshly earned, though it had gone so long without it.

It seemed the few seconds of open air clued Kit in to how uncomfortable he was, because he tried to snatch the warm cloth from Basie as soon as he was within snatching-reach. Basie slipped it behind his back in a flash.

"I said I'd take care of you. Let me," Basie entreated.

Kit dropped his hand into his lap and nodded.

While Basie wiped Kit's skin clean, they chatted quietly about Basie's trip back home and about Kit's work at the bakery. Basie listened to Kit detail all the shenanigans the folks in town had gotten mixed up in, and listened some more when he realized he didn't have his own to share.

Eventually, they were a dozen stories, a set of clean sheets, and one forgotten shower cap into the afternoon. Kit's head was laid on Basie's chest, and he grazed his nails through the soft patch of chest hair in tiny strokes. It was nice to catch up, but it was also nice to simply…lie there.

"I take back what I said," Basie decided, looking up at nothing. "It *was* exactly right."

"What was?"

That was how Basie knew he did his job right—Kit didn't remember how worried he'd been.

"This," replied Basie, gesturing between the bare skin and sweat of their bodies. "Us."

Kit made a sound of understanding, laying his chin on Basie's chest.

"It was." A small smile. "It is."

Great Day in the Morning

A "What If" Story

THE COTTAGE AT 6163 Annadale Drive was exactly one hour and thirty-seven minutes from Kit Elliot's old apartment in Baltimore. It was a pleasant drive, one where you really had to enjoy the sight of pine trees and hills to get the full effect. But Kit, during the few glances he stole away from the road, could see what was really there. Narrow dirt lanes that led to farm houses people called home. A thousand lookout points at which you could pull the car over and see the expanse of forever laid out before you.

And a town called Long Lily, a place nestled in the Pennsylvanian tip of Appalachia that he'd found on an envelope and hadn't been able to shake.

Kit clutched his hands on the wheel, glancing in the rearview mirror at the Maryland U-Haul hitched to the back of his old van. He still couldn't believe he was doing this. He'd been going through his things, starting to pack for a destination he hadn't yet discovered, when the empty envelope had slipped out from the musty pages of an old book. There was a crease along the top resulting from the envelope's many years as a bookmark, but he could still make out the return address and the name scrawled in old-fashioned cursive: *Della Yeats.*

Under normal circumstances, Kit was not in the habit of writing letters to strangers. But there'd been something about that name. Something about that specific address and its second line: *Wellhead Cottage.* He wanted to know it. More importantly, he wanted to know if he could find a place that could belong to him and feel the way the words *Wellhead Cottage* made him feel.

So he wrote to Della Yeats—adding "Ms." before her name so as not to seem impolite—and asked her to describe Long Lily. He wrote that he was sorry, but he could not remember why they had written to each other in the first place. He told her about his landlord wanting to sell the complex. How he'd been wanting to get out of Baltimore for some time now and could she please tell him what Long Lily was like so that he may consider it as a contender for places to move to. He even signed his full, Christian name, even though he was far past the point of enjoying when people called him Christopher.

His heart had nearly jumped out of his chest when he'd found her reply sitting on top of his pile of utility bills. The letter was simple:

"If you want to know what it's like, come stay with us. We'll find you a house. You already have the address, so come when you please. Bring your things. —Della"

Kit's letter in return had been just as concise. He'd be there in two weeks.

Now, those two weeks were up and Kit was somewhere so much greener. He couldn't remember much about leaving Maryland—only that Tom Petty had been singing through the radio about wildflowers and home as Kit had crossed the state line. The hours in between had been a haze.

Long Lily was only a few miles away now.

★★★

I T WASN'T THAT KIT was unfamiliar with the presence of magic. He came from a long line of faeries who had once incorporated magic into their daily lives the way humans now used the internet. But never before had he found himself among magic that desperately wanted to be known. It'd enveloped him at his first step out of the van, nuzzling against his legs and hands like a dog excited to see a familiar face. Kit looked around the yard. Everything seemed normal, from the regal willow tree along the creek to the well-tended garden of sunflowers and herbs. Maybe Della Yeats didn't realize that there was something *more* thriving under her soil. Or maybe she did.

The magic only seemed to grow stronger as he made his way up to the front door. In her most recent letter, Della had told Kit to just let himself in. Maybe it was because he'd spent the last generation of his life in a city, but there was *no way* he was going to let himself into someone else's home. He pulled the sleeve of his dress shirt down in a nervous habit, then politely knocked on the door.

If Kit was 103, his intuition was older. It was a living thing forged before he was born and placed like a spirit in his body to keep him out of harm. He trusted it before all else. When a man with sun on his breath opened the door, Kit's intuition said: *He is the man all this has been for.* Kit listened, because there was no choice—he couldn't look away from the man if he tried. Maybe there was something to it, because the man's gaze on him was just as heavy.

"Ah, Mr. Baltimore himself arrived from his long trek across state lines. Mom is wrist deep in the garden out back, so she sent me to get the door. Hence the—" The man gestured down at his overalls, which were unclasped and hanging around his waist. "Anyways, come on in."

"Thanks," Kit said, taking a sheepish step inside. His chest gave a squeeze as the man reached around him to shut the door. He took off down the hall, nodding for Kit to follow him.

"Sorry about the heat. I know it's not much cooler inside. We open the windows in the morning and close them when the sun rises to trap in what little fresh air we can get, but sometimes it's not much of a help." As he led Kit up the hallway into the cottage's kitchen, Kit could see patches of damp on the man's shirt where his sweat was still drying. The man paused, giving a quick glance over his shoulder. "I'm Basie. Like the jazz musician."

Kit had to smile. He'd seen Count Basie live at Wringley Field in 1945, just days after he made it back from serving overseas. In his opinion, the name was fitting, for all that Basie's voice sounded like music—smooth and confident. Kit had a strange urge to make some pun about Count Basie songs, like *Why don't you fly me to the moon, 'lil darling,* but he'd have sooner died than *actually* say it.

Rather, he said, "I'm Kit Elliot. Named after a rather crotchety grandfather, I'm afraid."

Basie smirked the way people do when they've decided to give the gift of their approval.

"Glad to see the grumpy gene skipped a few generations." Basie nodded at the back door. "My ma will be wanting to meet you. We've been out back all morning planting an army's worth of cucumber seeds. Someone in town swore they'd win the gold ribbon for pickles at the fair this year, so now she's determined to get them started early and perfect her recipe. Personally, I think that's an overreaction, but what do I know? I'm just the electrician."

"The longer they sit in the pantry, the better the flavor is!" came a voice from the backyard.

Kit followed Basie through the screen door to the back patio, where Della Yeats was still kneeling in the soil, thumbing seeds into the ground. She looked up at the men on her porch, shielding her eyes with a dirt-covered hand, then let out a cry of delight. She scurried across the yard with little regard for the mason jar of seeds she'd kicked over in her haste.

"Ma, the cucumbers," Basie groused.

"Damn the cucumbers!" She enveloped Kit in her arms before he could open his, but had enough consideration to hold her soiled hands away from his dress shirt. She pulled back, wiping her palms on her gardening apron. "Christopher Elliot, you are just as lovely in person as your art. Welcome to Wellhead Cottage."

"Thank you, Miss Della. It's beautiful here. And, just Kit is fine."

Della beamed.

"How was your trip? Has Basie offered you something to drink? Are you hungry? Have you had lunch yet?"

Kit floundered with what question to answer first, tossing a pleading look at Basie.

"Tell you what," Basie said. He picked up the hose and rinsed the remaining dirt off his own hands. "Let's all go inside. I'll make sandwiches and poor Kit can tell you all about his long, treacherous journey."

It turned out that the recipe for the sandwiches came from Lewie Simon's little sister, who wanted to know if she was onto something with her unique creation.

"You can be honest if they're terrible and I'll just make you a couple of grilled cheeses," Basie murmured into Kit's ear. The conspiratorial gesture shouldn't have brought chills up Kit's arm, but it did, so he hid his hands under the table.

Kit remembered that Lewie Simon was the man he'd been emailing for months about house tours and property investments. Finding out that Basie knew the town's main Realtor gave Kit hope that he might actually find somewhere to live, after all. The longer he was here, the more he wondered if possibly Basie and Della knew *everybody* in Long Lily.

"So, Kit, what's your plan for your stay?" Della asked, bringing a glass of ice water to her lips. "You're welcome here as long as you like, but I did promise I'd help show you around."

"I've got a few house tours scheduled with Lewie starting tomorrow. I'll probably put a good offer on whichever one I like best and move in as soon as they'll let me."

"Is this your first house?"

It shouldn't have been. Kit had been alive long enough to have five houses, but since he'd always lived alone and traveled so frequently, he'd always just rented. Or crashed on couches. Or sometimes even slept in his car.

"It is," he admitted. "But I'm not picky. And I imagine I can learn how to HGTV a home into something I can tolerate."

"*Tolerate*," Della scoffed. "We can do better than tolerate. You're in luck. I flipped this place from a church into a cottage. I'll help you, and I'm sure the folks in town will lend a hand too."

They would? The thought ought not to have troubled Kit, but could he really take advantage of his neighbors' kindness like that? He couldn't keep track of all the places he'd lived in his life, but he knew for a fact that he hadn't ever helped any of his neighbors renovate their houses.

"What properties are you looking at?" Basie cut in.

Kit pulled out a small notebook from his pocket and flipped it open.

"Tomorrow, I'm looking at some place called 'the old Murphey house.' Then the day after that, Lewie is taking me into town to look at a property on Collins Drive and—"

Before Kit could finish, Basie had whipped the landline off its hook—a rotary phone with wires that looked like they'd been combed the wrong way by a bad hairdresser—and dialed a number from memory. He held the phone between his shoulder and his ear, tearing a piece of cheese off his sandwich and tossing it into his mouth.

Kit hadn't even heard a quiet *Hello?* from the phone's speakers before Basie was asking, "Now, why on earth are you showing Kit Elliot the Murphy house? I wouldn't put my worst enemy in that dump."

"I don't mind at least looking at them," Kit tried to chime in, but Della only smiled and shook her head at him.

Basie hopped up on the counter, face incredulous. If he heard Kit at all, he was ignoring him.

"...Because I've seen the electrical work in that place, Lew," he continued. "You'd have to tear all the walls out just to make it safe to live. That house on Collins is no good either—" Basie cut off, pulling the phone away to look at it as if it had insulted him. A tinny voice came ranting through the device, but Basie pulled it back up to his ear with a scowl. "You know what, I will."

Basie slammed the phone onto its base, looked Kit dead in the eye, and said, "*I'm* going to show you around."

"You *are?*" Della chimed in with a disbelieving laugh.

Basie ignored her.

"If you're going to live here, you want someplace unique. You want someplace that when you're dead and gone, they'll say *Oh, that was Kit Elliot's place. What a great man he was.* And not, *Oh, that was Kit Elliot's place. They had to tear it down because it was already half falling apart when he got it and now there ain't nothing left.*"

"Glad you're thinking ahead," said Della sarcastically, though the glint in her oak eyes revealed she was tickled pink. She glanced at Kit from over her teacup. "But he's right. You don't want to tie yourself to the wrong house forever."

"It wouldn't be *forever,*" Kit insisted. He was thankful he had a hundred years of lying to make the fib sound halfway believable. Della looked down at her tea and sipped. "I could always move again if it really isn't a good fit."

"I thought the whole point of you coming here was to find someplace permanent to settle," Della wondered.

"Well, it *was,* but—"

"Then what's the problem with taking the time to find somewhere you *fit* with?"

"I don't want Basie to have to go to all that trouble. I'm sure the houses Lewie has picked out are more than fine."

Basie hopped off of the island counter and poured himself a mug of lukewarm coffee.

"That's really thoughtful of you," he said, "but I've already declared war with my best friend and now I gotta see it through. He'll never shut up about it otherwise." Basie opened the junk drawer and pulled out a pen and a pad of paper. He began to scribble something down, like he was afraid he'd forget it if he waited a second longer.

"Besides," Basie said while he wrote, "there's no one in Long Lily that knows this town better than I do. Not even Lewie. You're in a professional's hands."

If Kit didn't know any better, he'd say he heard a suggestion of…*something* in Basie's voice.

Willing the warmth on his face to cool, Kit replied. "Well, in that case, show me what you got."

Basie grinned.

★★★

K IT ELLIOT WAS AN observant man. He'd taken note of many things in his first few hours at Wellhead Cottage. Though, where he would usually give himself a silent pat on the back for catching those hard-to-reach perceptions, he found the Yeats family were exactly who they said they were—unabashedly transparent. They were honest people who found irreplaceable value in these few acres of land. And, to Kit's piqued interest, they were evenly as observant as he was. Just that same night, Basie had shown Kit around his own bedroom—the place Kit would be staying. Basie must've cleaned it before Kit arrived, but it seemed like Basie had removed all of his pictures from his dresser and the wall. He probably thought Kit would be uncomfortable at having to stare up at strange faces all night, which was a courtesy no one else in Kit's life would've considered—if not a strange one. Once Kit was in his pajamas reading, sitting up underneath a thin quilted blanket, Basie knocked on the door. Kit called for him to enter, but Basie only stuck his head and arm in enough to place a steaming mug on the bedside table.

Kit lifted the mug under his nose and inhaled.

"How on earth did you know?" he asked, unable to hide his surprised delight.

Basie shrugged.

"You seem like a lavender tea at night kind of guy. Sleep well," he replied.

He was gone before Kit could tell him how thoughtful the gesture was. If he'd lingered for a little while longer, Kit might have worked up the nerve to invite Basie in for a late-night chat. He found people's hearts were loosest before bed—you could look inside and get to the true root of them without causing alarm. For some reason—be it the loveliness of Basie's smile or his own pressing curiosity—Kit wanted to know who Basie was underneath his electrician clothes and small town skin.

The warmth of Basie's gesture carried on into the sleepless night as Kit laid awake in thought.

There was an old spirit about the cottage that Kit could not put his finger on. It was hard to say whether it was from Della's quiet wisdom, Basie's quick wit, or the old wooden walls themselves that creaked like a human pulse. Time was not important here, so Kit allowed himself to enjoy the endless hours of the evening. Maybe it was the first time he'd ever ignored the ticking of his watch, which was strange considering how little cause there was for him to rush.

Then, out in the hallway, footsteps passed Kit's bedroom. They were slow and creaky enough to make any mortal child fear for ghosts, but Kit figured if he hadn't made a ghost's acquaintance yet, it wasn't going to happen. Whoever it was let themselves into the bathroom and reemerged a few minutes later. Only they lingered in front of Kit's door.

Another knock.

Kit was careful to keep his voice quiet, "Come in."

It was Basie. He appeared in the golden lamp light beside Kit's bed, hair messy, like he'd been tossing and turning on the couch downstairs.

"Saw you had the light on. Can't sleep?" he asked.

Kit wasn't sure how to explain that no, he couldn't, but he didn't mind being awake. Basie continued before he could figure out how.

"If we're both up, can I come in?"

If Kit was drowsy before, now he was perfectly awake. Everything in him recognized that this was a man to pay attention to. Besides, if he was going to be up in the middle of the night, he might as well have company.

Kit nodded at Basie. He might've welcomed him in with words, but when he saw that Basie was only wearing loose boxers, his mouth ran dry.

Basie plopped down into an armchair by the window, curling

his legs up underneath his chin. Moonlight spilled in through the casement, illuminating one side of Basie's face in heavenly silver.

"It's bleeding hot in here," Basie said.

"Open the window then," replied Kit, smiling.

Basie did. A lilting breeze drifted into the room, carrying with it a pleasant chill and a long silence.

"So," started Basie when neither of them had said anything for too long. "What's got you up? If you're afraid of monsters under the bed, I promise it's safe. I've checked a hundred times for them. Unless you've got a phobia for dust bunnies—in which case, you better escape while you can."

Kit chuckled lowly. "Do you ever have a hard time sleeping because you're *too* comfortable?"

Basie tilted his head back.

"Oh, don't say that. My mom will want to move you right in and then you'll never have a place of your own." He met Kit's gaze through his lashes. "Not that you wouldn't be welcome. My ma seems like she's over-hospitable, but really, she just loves good company. And, boy, does she like you. At dinner, you made her laugh harder than anyone has in years. She's heard every joke there is to tell."

Kit grinned, placing his book on the bedside table to give Basie his complete attention.

"Well, I like her too. Both of you. I think there are some people that you *fit* with; no effort required."

"There's a word for that, you know." When Kit lifted a brow, Basie corrected, "Actually, there's probably plenty of words for it. But the one I know is from—" He scoffed. "It's from *Anne of Green Gables* of all things. My mom's got a collection of first editions downstairs. There's a part in one of the books where an old man living by Anne's house tells her she belongs to 'The Race That Knows Joseph' because they get along so well."

Kit cocked his head.

"Who's Joseph?"

"Hell if I know. Point is, you do know Joseph—even if you don't *know* him—and it means you've got friends for life outta me and my mom, no matter where you go."

It didn't make a lick of sense, but Kit found he didn't need it to. He still understood.

"What about you?" he asked, resting his chin on his own knee. "You make it sound like you'll be living with your mom for the rest of your life."

"Some people do that, you know. They live with their families all their lives." Basie turned his face toward the window. "I like it here. If I ever find a man willing to start a family in this tiny cottage with my mom, then it'll be more than just the two of us. But I know all the eligible men in town, and they're not really my type. But who knows? Maybe a miracle will happen."

"Well, actually…" Kit tried to keep his voice light. "As soon as I find a place, the number of gay men in Long Lily will have increased by one."

Basie stared at Kit, lips parted, like he couldn't believe Kit was flirting at 3:13 in the morning. Kit could hardly believe it either. But then, he'd been the one to say that hearts were more unbound in the witching hours.

"Oh," said Basie dumbly. "I—"

The red-faced floundering was how Kit knew flirting hadn't been a terrible idea. He'd been nervous, at first. After all, they'd known each other less than a full turn of the earth. But maybe it wasn't a bad idea to let himself cast the idea to Basie and let him decide what to do with it.

"We have to find you a house first," Basie managed to say, hiding his face behind his palm. "Somewhere good."

"I appreciate your determination to match me with the perfect residence, though I have to admit, I still don't understand it."

A strange expression crossed Basie's face—one people wear when they expect to sound like they've lost their mind.

"I just…noticed that if people can find a home where they *really* belong, they have better lives. It's like picking out a pet. You can't just trust any old dog at the pound. You have to hold each one in your arms, look into its eyes, and see if it has the capacity to love you."

"We're still talking about houses, right?"

Basie scoffed, rolling his eyes.

"We're talking about *belonging*, Kit. If you pick somewhere you don't belong, you're going to spend your entire life thinking *you're* the reason you don't feel settled. All the work and effort and soul you pour into the place will all be wasted, and you'll be miserable."

Kit mulled the words over.

"What if it was you?" he asked.

Basie's brows nudged together.

"What if what was me?"

"If you had to move out of Wellhead Cottage and find somewhere else in Long Lily, where would you go?"

The man hesitated in the summery moonlight. Perhaps he had never considered that he could belong anywhere other than this small patch of land among ancient mountains and familiar faces. Basie stood, the floors creaking as he padded across the room and sat on the edge of the bed. The mattress dipped under his weight.

Kit recalled the last few times he'd shared a bed with someone—how the warmth and density of another man beside him had always felt like a foreign entity. Not entirely real. But Basie's presence was familiar somehow, making the bed even more comfortable than before, even when he was nearly sitting at his feet.

"Would you like me to show you?" Basie asked carefully. "Tomorrow, when I show you different properties, I can take you there."

I'd let you show me anything, Kit wanted to say. Instead, he let loose another small smile and looked at Basie's fingers on the bed.

"You make house hunting sound like an adventure," Kit said lightly.

The bed creaked again and Basie was gone, back in the doorway. Golden light from the bedside lamp casted onto him, revealing another rosy flush along his collarbones and down over his heart.

"You should rest. You had a big day and today is just the start," Basie whispered.

"As you say." Around them the night let out a sigh. "Goodnight, Basie."

★★★

IN THE MORNING, KIT woke to the smell of fresh eggs and toast lofting from the kitchen. He thought he remembered hearing hushed murmuring earlier the same morning, but he must've fallen back asleep. Kit yawned, pushing up onto his elbows to check the clock across the room. A little swell of disquiet bloomed in Kit's core—the same uncomfortable feeling that came any time his routine was disrupted. He'd never slept this late before. It was a wonder the Yeatses had waited this long before starting breakfast. At this point, it was practically lunch.

After dressing in his favorite olive linen pants and freshening up, Kit followed the steps downstairs in the kitchen. Basie stood at the stove, flipping eggs with a strong shove of his pan. A bead of oil popped off the hot skillet, landing on his knuckle. Basie wiped his hand on the daffodil towel flung over his shoulder and hissed.

"Goddamned eggs can't stay in the pan without trying to kill me," he grumbled.

Kit folded his arms behind his back.

"...Everything alright?" he asked, just as another pop of oil shot from the pan.

"Great day—!" Basie cursed, slamming the skillet back onto the burner. For a second, Kit thought he'd upset Basie, but the man was heaving out laughter in no time.

"Is it...really a great day?" Kit asked, sneaking around Basie to turn the heat down on the stove. This only made Basie's smile grow.

"It's just a saying. Probably more of a curse when it's coming out of my mouth," Basie explained. He slid the eggs onto a plate, sprinkled some fresh cheese overtop the orange yolks, then ran the top of his hand under the cold water of the sink. "If you're not hungry, then you better do laps around the yard until you *are* hungry, because there is a *lot* of food."

Kit lifted his shoulders shyly, leaning against the counter. "I hope you weren't waiting for me. You would've been fine eating without me."

"Not at all. We sleep in and then do big breakfasts on Saturdays. Normally Lewie comes with the kids, but one of the girls is apparently having a crisis after trying to use acrylic paint as hair dye. Just as well. The kids are…" Basie whistled. "Delightful, intelligent little beasts. But they're a lot." Basie gestured at the kitchen table. "My mom's just up the road buying maple syrup from our neighbors. Mrs. Mallory makes better syrup than anything you've tried. Why don't you have a seat?"

Kit glanced around at the dishes piling up in the sink, then at the unsqueezed oranges next to an empty pitcher.

"There has to be something I can do to help. I'll feel awful just sitting watching you."

Basie jabbed the spatula at the chair.

"No sir. Make like an autumn leaf and sit your butt down."

Kit obeyed. He thought that if Basie had asked him to cover himself in maple syrup and chicken feathers, he would've asked, *How many?* The idea of it made Kit nervous. He was not the sort to be addlebrained over handsome men he'd only met a day ago. It reminded him of being young—nearly a hundred years ago. Of the very first dreams he'd had of wrapping himself in a man's arms and tasting lips and sweat and velvet. At his age, he let his interest grow only during the wisest occasions. Since he was immortal, these *wise occasions* came as slowly as his own aging.

But it grew now. It grew as he chatted with Basie about all the things people talked about when they barely knew each other.

Over the course of his life, these types of conversations occupied most of Kit's speech with other people. Giving an abridged truth about himself over and over had proved duller with each passing year. Yet, this couldn't have been further from the case talking with Basie, who drank up everything Kit said with keen interest.

In the short half hour Kit watched Basie flip eggs and squeeze oranges, he'd learned that Basie had played baseball in high school on the Long Lily team, was currently tutoring all of Lewie's kids in Spanish, and had never—not once—met his father. In return, Kit had told Basie that while he'd never been an athlete, he had a keen hand for baking and painting. He told Basie that he was somewhat of a linguist— "You're fluent in *how many* languages?—and for what it was worth, he didn't remember the last time he'd spoken to his father, either.

Basie had paused then, gazing over at Kit as if he were looking at something new for the very first time. The air between them fizzed, primed to ignite if either of them said the wrong thing—or, maybe not the *wrong* thing, but the thing that would make this real. The catalyst to bring their connection into existence, impossible to ignore.

But then Della was bursting through the front door, yelling about how *Lynn Mallory is too old to be this stubborn about letting someone else take over the sugaring for her,* and the tension evaporated like hot breath on cold air.

Kit couldn't remember the last time breakfast had been so pleasant. He'd thought his own breakfast traditions—a coffee, a toasted bagel, and a freshly inked newspaper—were the height of luxury. But there was something *more* about sitting round a handmade dining room table with enough food to feed a king, laughing and joking like it was the only thing any of them were put on the earth to do. Della was a skilled conversationalist, almost too good for Kit to keep up with. The only thing that kept him afloat was Basie, who was there every step of the way, explaining what needed elaboration and slowing her down when she got excited. When his plate was just crumbs and smears of maple syrup, Kit had a passing thought that this dining room might've been the brightest place in all the world.

"We ought to get going," Basie groaned, one hand on his full belly. "Apparently Jed Donlevy has a hive of bees all mixed up with his electrical and I promised him I'd come take a look before the end of the day. Poor Elise has been getting stung in her sleep."

Della downed the rest of her coffee, sitting back in her chair with an expression of contentment.

"Take your suit. And, for God's sake, charge the man for your services! You've got to be the only man this side of the mountains that can handle something like that, but you never let anyone pay you!"

Basie made a series of noncommittal noises that likely amounted to *Ehhh, I probably most likely definitely certainly won't be doing that.* Della shook her head and started collecting the plates.

By the time Basie was herding Kit out the door, he had stuffed his arms with large umbrellas.

"What are those for? It's completely sunny out," Kit wondered.

Basie flipped the umbrellas over his shoulder with enough grace to give Gene Kelly a run for his money.

"You'll see."

It wasn't until Kit was buckled in Basie's '85 Ford F150 that he discovered their first destination: a nook at the crown of Long

Lily called Crane's Nest. The property was apparently within walking distance, though Basie insisted on driving. He'd gone to the trouble of changing the radio to music Kit liked, even though the commute was shorter than the length of the song playing over the speakers.

As soon as they crossed into Crane's Nest, Kit became thankful for the umbrella he was clutching in his hands. He'd somehow missed sight of where the dark rain clouds began, but as the truck crossed under the canopy of forest trees, a violent downpour began to spill over the truck. It pattered on the roof, the sound of a thousand tiny pebbles against metal. Kit wasn't sure how Basie could see the road—maybe he just knew where he was going, but eventually the truck rolled up to an old building. It wasn't until Kit unfurled his umbrella and braved the first step out of the truck that he realized he was looking at an old diner.

"This is it," Basie said, speaking loud enough to be heard over the rain. He couldn't quite get his own umbrella open, so Kit darted over to him and held it above both their heads.

Kit looked down. Basie was shorter than him, but not by much. Still, under the safety of the umbrella, Basie was close enough to feel his breath. Water dripped from the curly ends of his hair and his long lashes. It dripped down the side of his face, begging to be swept aside. Kit gripped the umbrella tighter, holding back the urge.

Basie looked Kit up and down.

"I should've told you not to wear your nice shoes."

Kit scoffed, trying not to smile.

"I only own nice shoes." He nodded at the diner, squinting across the lot at the main entrance. "You want me to move in *here?*"

"You wanted to know where I would live if I could choose anywhere in Long Lily. If all the conditions were perfect, this is where I would choose."

The conditions were obviously *not* perfect. Even without the rain, the diner was in terrible shape. It was missing too many siding panels and most of the windows were broken clean through. It looked so much like it had survived the end of the world, that Kit's imagination was not clever enough to conjure what it might've looked like in its proper glory. It was for this reason Kit turned to Basie and said, "Show me."

To Kit's surprise, Basie opened the front door without needing a key. He held it open for Kit to slip inside. Kit did, pulling the umbrella shut and shaking the excess water out over the debris covered ground.

"Have you got a sixth sense for rain or something?" Kit wondered, leaning the umbrella against the door.

"Oh, it's always raining here."

"Right." Kit crossed his arms over his chest, the draft from the cracked windows falling cool over where his shirt had gotten damp. He looked over the space. It definitely had been a diner—once. Splitting booth seats lay haphazardly along the walls, foam spilling out of their cracks like blood from a wound. The floors were stained from rust that must've dripped from places Kit couldn't originate. "Not exactly the pinnacle of interior design. You're sure *this* is where you would live?"

"Trust the process, Baltimore," Basie replied. He sauntered up to the milkshake counter, pulled a rag from the inside of his electrician coveralls, and wiped the surface clean—or, as clean as it could be, considering. With ease, he hoisted himself up onto the counter, patting the seat next to him. "Let me paint you a picture."

Although Kit was wary of what manner of strange substances still lingered on the counter's surface, Kit boosted himself up with the footrest of the spinning barstool. He sat next to Basie, muscles stiff. The length of his arm ran along Basie's, creating a sort of give and take of warmth. Kit laid his hands flat on his thighs, like the sensation of touching Basie had shocked him into stillness.

Basie nudged an elbow into Kit's side.

"The place isn't going to bite you. Relax a little."

Kit did, infinitesimally.

"Look, there are good bones here. You just have to picture them."

Kit didn't see bones anywhere, much less good ones, but he let Basie paint the picture.

"I'd take out all those small, cracked up windows and replace them with bigger ones. In the woods, you need all the light you can get, you know? Half of the counter would go, but I'd leave a little bit up. Like a classy little bar."

"For classy little drinks?" Kit wondered, trying his best to play along.

"For *classy little drinks*," Basie agreed emphatically. "The place already has a kitchen and a bathroom, so that's easy. With half the counter gone, that's plenty of space to throw up a wall and make a bedroom-for-one."

"Just one?"

"Sure."

"Your dream house situation includes a life of solitude? That sounds awfully lonely."

Basie paused. He looked at Kit from the corner of his eye, the light dimming out of his expression.

"How can you be lonely when you're surrounded by a hundred of your closest tree friends?" he laughed, but Kit saw it for the artful dodge it was. "It's peaceful out here. If I get really desperate for company, Jed's just on the other side of the creek and he's always looking for someone to speak loudly at."

"You really wouldn't live here with anyone else?"

"Who would I live with?"

A strange, uncomfortable feeling came over Kit—like wearing wet socks or accidentally scratching a nail on a chalkboard. The question had spurred a thousand answers within Kit, all at war with one another. *You'd live with me, of course* butted heads against *Definitely* not *me, I couldn't ever see myself living here.* Then those two turned their weapons to, *Why am I even considering myself part of the equation? You're practically a stranger?* Which was already sparring with, *I feel like I've known you every day of my one hundred years.*

"Not terribly prone to falling in love, then?" Kit wondered lightly.

"Not terribly, no," Basie replied. But there was…something in his gaze. Something that grabbed Kit by the underside of his jaw and made him *look.*

And he did—look, that is. He poured every ounce of his attention to staring down at Basie. The deep dip at the heart of his lips. The way his tan skin managed to catch every spare ray of light that it could wrangle from the dim dining room. The damp curls of his hair still sending drops of rain down his temple.

One of the drops ran down Basie's nose, lingering over the swell of his lips. Kit followed the movement, burning and burning, until all the conflict in his head was just ash and smoke.

Kit jolted back, clearing his throat.

"W-what about the rain?"

Basie blinked, stalling like a flooded engine. When he seemed to reroute their conversation back on track, he blurted, "I'd stop it."

It was Kit's turn to be stunned.

"You can't *stop the rain,* Basie. Not unless you've got some sort of hidden magic I don't know about."

Like being one hundred and three years old and descending from faeries?

Basie's face did something strange, but he schooled his expression and bumped his shoulder against Kit's.

"That's why this is a hypothetical situation. If I could—damn, I don't know—control the lightning in the sky or some shit, I'd be one hell of an electrician."

Somehow, Kit got the impression that Basie was the next best thing and the people of Long Lily knew it.

He looked over the diner again and he saw it. The big windows. The cozy bedroom overlooking the pine tree heart of Crane's Nest. Even the classy little bar for classy little drinks.

"I think it's a good daydream," he said after a while. "I think it could be a good reality too if you ever really wanted it."

"That would mean Jed letting go of the property, which ain't gonna happen." Basie let out a long sigh and hopped off the counter. "But it's like you said. It'd be pretty damn lonely."

"Not with visitors."

Basie, who had made his way to the door to grab the umbrellas, slowly turned around. His expression was hopeful, and maybe a little curious.

"You tellin' me you'd visit me, Kit Elliot?"

I'd do a lot more than visit you.

"Yeah, of course I'd visit you."

"Tell you what." Basie handed Kit the umbrella, trying without success to hold back a smile. "If I ever find a way to control the weather and give this diner the facelift it needs, you're welcome any time."

Kit held the umbrella atop Basie's fingers, letting the touch linger a second longer than it needed to.

Basie cleared his throat.

"I should show you the place I actually meant to take you," he murmured, cheeks warm. "After all, you're the one actually looking for a place to live."

★★★

Mallory Farm (*BERRIES AND dairies since 1920*) was up the hill from Wellhead Cottage. Driving past Wellhead to get to it, Kit could see how far the property extended into tall grass and orange tiger lilies. He wasn't expecting Basie to pull into a driveway that was so close to the cottage. And he *really* wasn't expecting for the yard to be void of any *For Sale* sign. But Basie insisted that this property was for sale, regardless of the way it seemed.

"Lynn raised her family here. She wants to keep running the business, but keeping up the house has been a beast of its own.

There's a smaller house a little further up the property that she's planning on moving to," Basie explained as they let themselves onto the driveway.

"Why not list the house with Lewie?"

"He's the Realtor, but Lynn didn't want to list the house anywhere but the papers. She wants the house to go to someone from Long Lily wanting to start a family."

Kit paused in the driveway. He didn't meet any of those qualifications—at least as far as Basie was concerned. He wasn't *opposed* to starting a family. It was something he'd thought about when he first started looking at houses. But Basie didn't know that.

Kit stuffed his hands in his pockets.

"Are you sure she'll even show me the house?" he asked.

It was at this point Basie seemed to realize what he had said. He came over to Kit, laying a hand on his arm.

"All I mean is, she doesn't want a complete stranger. You're a friend of mine, and no friend of mine is a stranger. Come on, I'll show you."

Kit didn't expect Basie to immediately put his money where his mouth was, but he did. Because instead of walking up the porch and knocking politely on the heavy stained-wood door, Basie jumped up the stairs and let himself right into the house.

"Lynn! I brought company! Can I come in?"

Kit lingered outside the threshold. He wouldn't step a foot into the house until he heard a concrete welcome.

"Sure, darlin'! I'm just in the kitchen."

Basie dragged Kit along, following the echoing of the voice through the house where a plump, tan woman was kneading pie dough on the counter. Her long brown hair was intricately braided, rounded on itself and pinned to the top of her hair in a pretty bun. Basie waltzed right into the kitchen, turned down the radio, and pressed a kiss to Lynn's cheek. She leaned up into it, placing a kiss of her own on Basie's cheek. When she noticed Kit, her expression brightened.

"My word! And who is this fellow?" she asked. She said *this* like it secretly came with some type of descriptor. Kit couldn't catch the meaning. *Tall* fellow? Freckled fellow? "I'd shake your hand, but uh…"

She held up two flour-covered hands. Basie grinned and placed a hand on Kit's shoulder.

"Lynn Mallory, this is Kit Elliot, Long Lily's newest resident."

"Just as soon as we find somewhere for me to live," Kit interjected shyly.

"Oh, I see. You're here to see the house. What I can tell you from here is that it's four beds, two and a half baths, and a grand old backyard." Lynn hissed. She pulled her hands away from the dough and massaged her wrists, eyebrows knitting together. "Son of a bitch. Sorry, my carpal tunnel is acting up and it makes this a little tougher."

Then, to Kit's horror, she started kneading the dough *some more*.

"Anyways, the house is awfully lonely since my husband passed away last winter," Lynn continued. "With all the kids moved out, the only people I see are my staff in the barns, and…" Another hiss of pain. "I've figured out the things I need. This house isn't one of them. I still want the business. To see my neighbors every day."

It was the third wheeze of pain that finally did it.

"I can't watch this anymore," Kit exclaimed. He rounded the kitchen island and looked Lynn directly in the eyes. "Let me help you. I can be trusted with a pie, I promise. I won't overwork it. I'm not trying to show you how to do it—you clearly know what you're doing. Just give your poor wrists a break."

Lynn held his gaze for a long second, then threw the dough on the counter and sighed with resignation. A cloud of flour puffed up like a halo around the pie dough.

"You make a compelling argument," she relented.

Kit did not need to be told twice. He rolled up his sleeves and hurried over to the sink. With warm water, soap, and tenacity, he scrubbed the residual Crane's Nest dirt and mud from his hands. When they were dry, he gestured for Lynn to take the seat at the island next to Basie and got to work.

Sometimes, Kit thought that if anything were to happen to him and he got amnesia, he probably wouldn't be able to recover one hundred years' worth of memories—*but,* even in death, Kit Elliot would know how to make a pie. Lynn seemed poised to correct him and coach him through the process, but every time she opened her mouth, she decided to remain silent.

"Where are you from, Kit?" Lynn asked.

Maybe he was too distracted from rolling out the dough to the perfect thickness, or maybe he just felt comfortable, because Kit answered without hesitation.

"Ireland." The word slipped out before he could stop it. He paused, looking up just in time to see Basie's nose scrunch in confusion. "I mean, I've lived in plenty of places around the world. But I am Irish."

A few lifetimes ago, he'd even had Irish citizenship. But then he'd moved to the US with his parents where it was easier to get lost in the overflowing population of people. Besides, conveniently, he knew the immortals who worked in the Social Security office.

"So am I," Basie pointed out. "My ma's family is, at least. I've never been there."

"It's beautiful. The greenest place you've ever seen."

Kit draped the pie dough over the buttered pie dish. It was hand-painted in the center where someone had depicted bright sunflowers. He smoothed the dough down so it rested flat against the edges. He trimmed some of the excess away and melded it into other parts where the crust needed a little more umph. When there was an equal amount of dough along the entire perimeter, he began to crimp it. It came as easy and effortless as it always did.

He'd momentarily forgotten he had an audience when Lynn let out a low whistle.

"My goodness. You lookin' for a job, young man?"

It always tickled Kit when people called him *young man* when they were most certainly several generations younger than he was. He slid the finished pie dish across the table and grinned.

"As a matter of fact, ma'am, I will be. As soon as I can find somewhere to live."

Lynn pushed herself up, carrying in both weathered hands.

"Let me get this pie in the oven and then we'll see if I can convince you to buy the house and work in my bakery."

★★★

"A RE YOU *SURE* YOU don't want to look at any other houses?" Basie said emphatically as they walked back to Wellhead later that night. "It's not too late to call Lewie and have him show you the other places he had in mind."

"I'm certain," Kit stated resolutely. Certain didn't quite cover it. He'd never felt so assured about anything in his life. He was no stranger to moving on a whim, to picking the place that seemed like the best match on paper and committing to it because he should. But touring the Mallory farmhouse made Kit understand why he'd been wandering around the entire world, looking for somewhere that made him feel like *that.*

"I could *see* it, you know? Every time we entered a new room, I could picture the way my things would look in the cupboards. On the shelves. I'm thinking about turning that last bedroom into a library. You know, the one with all the bay windows? I could sew a cushion for it and sit there for hours."

Basie squinted up at Kit, partially blinded by the late afternoon sunshine. His smile was all wrinkly nose and lopsided lips.

"Excitement looks good on you," he commented.

"Oh, be quiet," Kit said, but he couldn't force the grin to leave his face. "I just—" He laughed, letting the sound echo into the fields of wildflowers and working honeybees. "I can't believe you knew me for one day and picked out exactly where I needed to be."

"Don't take this the wrong way, Kit, but you're not exactly a chapter in a book about oddities. You're exactly who you say you are. It didn't take a rocket scientist to figure out a place for you. Besides, Lynn's got those great ovens."

Kit let his face fall back, legs going soupy beneath him like he was drunk.

"I think I would've bought that leaky diner in Crane's Nest if it came with those *ovens,*" he swooned. "I'm already planning egg custard tarts and Cornish splits."

His feet scratched along the dirt road to a stop. All at once, the laughter was gone, and he looked straight into Basie's eyes like there was something secret and magic there to be discovered.

"Thank you," Kit said.

Basie flushed under the attention, waving an arm.

"It's nothing."

"It's not nothing," pressed Kit. "And you know it too."

Basie must've known because he didn't say anything. Kit almost wished he would. Wished that Basie would tell him that he'd go this far out of his way for any old neighbor—hell, maybe any stranger. At least, at that point, Kit could stop fooling himself that there was something there. Because as it stood, everything was falling perfectly into place. *Here, Kit Elliot, here is your perfect dream home sitting on the most lovely patch of land, shown to you by a man that makes you feel warm with every mile of your nerves.* Something was bound to fall through, and if it wasn't the house, then it had to be Basie.

Call him crazy—it'd been a whopping twenty-four hours—but Kit didn't want Basie to fall through.

★★★

THE RESIDENTS OF LONG LILY were like a storybook that never ran out of pages. In the days that Kit closed on the house and started moving all of his things into the Mallory

Farmhouse—which would remain the Mallory Farmhouse for as long as Kit lived in it—he met all his neighbors. Basie and Della were around the most, painting rooms that needed a fresh coat, making them bright and inviting. Della had taken to adding a mural in the dining room—the same one she had in her own bedroom that was based on Kit's long-ago sketch.

Sometimes Kit thought that they were inventing jobs as they went, looking for any excuse to sow their love into the renovations. Into every stained stretch of molding. Every breezy, hand-sewn curtain.

Kit did get to meet Lewie Simon eventually, who brought most of his legal wards with him to help move Lynn's things to her new home up the hill. Lewie, on the other hand, helped facilitate the completion of all the boring things, like the transfer of the deed.

Folks he couldn't have imagined seemed to pour from the woodwork, offering to steam floors, hang pictures, shelve books. Kit couldn't keep track of them all, mixing up names and blanking when he tried to call out to people. But they didn't mind. They only laughed, patted his shoulder, and reminded him: *I'm Emily Long.* Or, *I'm Frida Dixon.* And once, *I'll answer to anything, but just know I'm the one that pours your coffee at the diner, and you* don't *want to cross me.*

Kit baked everyone something sweet with his new ovens, even before he'd managed to get most of his own things unpacked.

When the house was ready to be filled, Basie took Kit out to the shed located in the Wellhead backyard. It'd been where they'd stored Kit's things after returning the moving trailer. Back then, Kit still played the role of *"guest,"* not the *"family member"* he'd somehow become, so Basie had taken care of storing the moving boxes himself. Now that Kit had started to assimilate into the community, even the tiny bit he had, Basie let Kit help with the unloading.

"What do you even keep in here?" Kit wondered, eyeing the strange boxes with even stranger years scribed onto their sides. The shed seemed to fit more than it looked like it could, another curious hint of magic Kit allowed himself to take note of.

"Oh, all the strange things my mother collects. Nothing terribly exciting," Basie answered.

Kit was too polite to wonder any further.

A few weeks later, when everything was finally unpacked, Kit had a passing thought that maybe he should hold onto the empty boxes like he always did—just in case he had to move again. But he didn't intend to, so he hosted a fire in his backyard and lit every one of those damned cardboard boxes into flames. Della and Basie had come over for the ceremonial bonfire. They sat shoulder-to-shoulder with their lawn chairs looking in the downwind direction to avoid smoke in their faces. Plumes of sooty gray and ignited ash lilted over the field into the tall grass like fireflies—bright on the descent, then disappearing into nothing.

Being around Basie hadn't become any easier, but as the weeks passed, Kit found he was not able to allow space between them. Their friendship was easy. At times, it was funny, the hardest Kit had laughed in decades. At other times, they shared secrets under low light, just like they had that first night. And all along, Kit's mind—the one that had lived and suffered and learned—warned him to be safe. To hold this new, fragile thing carefully. But

Kit's heart—the one that lived and suffered and loved—refused to listen.

Kit could feel Basie's presence beside him. He kicked his feet dangerously close to the fire, even though Della had scolded him not to. His face was gaping wide into the endless sea of stars above them. If Della hadn't been there, Kit might've told Basie what he knew of the constellations. It wasn't much, but lately he wanted to share *everything* he knew with Basie, like each piece of knowledge was a small gift.

"Kit, you hear me?"

He, in fact, had not heard Della calling his name over and over. Or, if he did, his mind had tuned it straight out. He turned his face away from where it had been ogling fairly obviously at Basie.

"No, sorry. What did you say?"

"I said there's been something I've been meaning to ask you about."

Kit straightened in his seat. Something in Della's tone was light and cautious. A tiny rush of adrenaline started coursing through Kit's chest, the kind that comes when you know something could go very, very badly, even if it doesn't look like it should.

"I'm an open book," he said earnestly.

Della's expression was hard to decipher across the firelight, but Kit found he couldn't look at her for long.

"I pulled out that first letter you wrote me. Well, it was a response to the one I wrote to you. About your piece in the magazine?"

Fear gave way to confusion.

"I remember that. You offered to pay me for the sketch. I was writing that I wouldn't accept your money."

"Exactly."

By now, Basie was looking at her strangely too, like he knew where this was going as little as Kit did.

"The date on that letter was March 11th, 1983."

Cold, icy dread fell over Kit.

This was it. That trepidation that had followed him around, warning him not to get comfortable, was finally here to collect payment.

How he had been so thoughtless? Had it really been so long since he'd first sent that letter? Time was a hard thing for him to hold anymore, but he thought he'd been…*aware* enough to differentiate his recent memories from the ones that had been born forty years ago.

But then, all at once, the memory sharpened into focus, like a camera lens turned to the right setting. He'd written the letter on a *typewriter* of all things. He'd signed it himself, but he was certain the paper had yellowed and worn. There'd be no denying it. Even if he wanted to, he'd have to lie and manipulate and deceive. He'd have to gaslight a woman he had nothing but love for and tell her that she was crazy, when she was horribly right.

In the midst of his mental panic, Kit realized that Basie had gone as still as death.

Kit couldn't lie. Not anymore. Maybe it was foolish, but he felt like he didn't need to. Here, watching his escape route go up in flames, Kit could only depend on Della Yeats being as good as she said she was.

"Yes," he said finally. "It was, wasn't it?"

Basie was the one to speak.

"But—You—Does that mean—"

That I descended from faeries and my life expectancy is at least 400 years old? Yes.

"How old are you, Kit Elliot?" Della asked quietly.

Kit's eyes slipped shut.

"Please don't ask me that."

"Kit," Basie said very, very carefully. "How old are you?"

A long sigh set loose from deep in Kit's lungs. Curse Basie Yeats and curse Kit's inability to tell him to mind his damn business.

"One hundred and three, I think."

"You *think?*"

Basie shot up out of his seat and started laughing hysterically, the way people do when they have to laugh, or they'll start clawing their hair out. Kit could imagine what Basie was thinking—that Kit was insane and he'd gone and invested all of his time into someone who thought they were immortal. Kit bolstered himself for the killing blow, reminding himself that it was only normal for Basie to assume the worst. The sting would hurt like a betrayal, but it was all normal. All completely, utterly normal.

Basie scrubbed his hands through his hair, then spun to Della.

"Wait a minute, you *knew?* This whole time? Since he showed up?"

Della shrugged.

"What was I supposed to say? *Hi Kit, you look* really *good for someone in their sixties?* I wanted Kit to have a chance to make his own decisions and settle down before I threw another wrench into the mix."

Kit blinked. He could count on one hand the number of instances over the course of his long life that he'd let his secret slip. He usually kept it like a stolen jewel in his pocket, one hand on it so he never fumbled it. Never let it slip from his grasp.

The most recent flub had been when his best friend from Maryland, Lara, had started going through the books on his shelf and found an old picture of him and Axe he'd accidentally used as a bookmark. That had gone fine—but only because Lara, the only child of an immigrant family, knew what it felt like to be the object of someone's misguided curiosity. There were still parts of him that couldn't forget the childhood stress and heartache of having to throw his things into whatever bag he could reach and flee his home. His parents had made it an art. Kit was tired of it.

He wouldn't pack up his house. He wouldn't leave Long Lily. Maybe he wouldn't have to. After all, Della had known all this time and hadn't thought any different of him.

But Basie…

"You should have told me," said Basie, to his mother of all people. Like it was Della's secret to tell.

Kit stood up, keeping his eyes stuck to the ground.

"I think I'm going to go inside," he said. He couldn't muster the usual warmth he carried in his words and his speech. "The hose is on if you want to put out the fire. But, uh, feel free to sit out as long as you'd like."

The harsh expression on Basie's face melted away as if he finally remembered Kit was still there.

"Wait a second. Kit. I didn't mean to—"

Kit held up his hands. "No, no. It's fine. Now you know. I just, whatever it makes you *think* of me—" The words cut off in a choke. *He thinks you're insane. And even if he believes you, he won't want to be involved with someone he thinks will live forever.* "Goodnight, everyone. Thanks for everything."

He didn't mean for it to sound like a long-term farewell, but it felt like one regardless. It couldn't be. The Yeats lived up the road and Kit had a feeling that Della wouldn't let him off the hook so easily. But for tonight, he could escape into the safe haven of his dark kitchen, sit on the floor against his ovens, and let the dread wash over him where he was safe to drown under it.

"*Kit,*" Basie pressed, but Kit was already half-way across the yard. He could feel Basie's stare on him as the thin dark of the night began to swallow him with each step away from the warm fire.

The last thing he heard before he was too far out of reach was Della sigh and say, "Now look what you've done."

When he was inside, Kit left all the lights off. He pulled the curtain away from the back window to watch the Yeats from the safety of his own living room. He watched all three times that Basie started marching up to the back door. He watched Basie lose his courage just as many times. He watched Della put out the fire, which was when he *stopped* watching.

The backyard was completely dark.

Usually when Kit was preoccupied with things he preferred not to fester in, he baked. But the house was too unfamiliar, his presence in it too new for the effect to be the same. He could lay in bed, but he still hadn't gotten used to the noises his old house made in the night—creaking walls and shifting floorboards. Instead, he decided to sit in his front parlor where the bay window overlooked the front yard and the dipping valley of perfectly quiet countryside.

Some time later, a figure appeared at the end of the drive. Kit wiped his eyes, wondering if the hazy film over his vision was making him see things. A shimmering stalk of moonlight. A strong wind carrying a swirl of last autumn's dead leaves. But the clouds parted enough for the moon to pour over the shadow.

It was Basie. He was carrying a small box underneath one arm, marching up the driveway like it was a matter of life or death.

The moment Basie's footsteps advanced up the porch, Kit crept off of the window seat until he was on the floor, peering over the edge and out the bay window.

Basie knocked. Kit, who could only see the back side of Basie's body, flinched, falling back onto his haunches. The banging echoed across the house, the emptiness of all the rooms making it louder than it probably was.

Another knock, followed by Basie's voice through the door, "I know you're in there. I saw you in the window."

Kit sat on the floor—caught. He knew he should stand up and face Basie like the level-headed, responsible person he was, but his muscles refused to comply with his demands.

"*Oh,* for the love of—I'm coming in!" Basie opened the door and stuck his head in. When he caught sight of Kit hunkered down on the floor, he frowned. "What in God's green earth are you doing there?"

"Waiting for you to go home," Kit answered quietly, making no attempt to stand up.

"You'll be waiting a long time. Or you could speed up the process by letting me apologize. I'll be sitting out on the porch until you're ready." He glanced outside. "But try not to wait too long. The Pennsylvania coyotes can smell desperation."

With that, he disappeared, closing the door behind him. Kit looked down at his knees, still bent in strange ways after his hasty escape from the window. The longer he sat here, the more ridiculous he felt. He should just go to bed—let all the chemicals in his head recharge and give him a clear mind in the morning. Unfortunately, he believed Basie's threat to wait on the porch as long as it took.

Drawing in a long sigh, Kit slowly crept out the front door. Basie was sitting on the stairs, legs stretched out onto the lower steps as he leaned on his elbows. His eyes, which he had been resting, slipped open, but he didn't turn around to face the man lingering in the doorframe.

"If you think I've lost my mind, you better tell me now," Kit said sternly. His knuckles were bone white as they clutched the door handle, ready to bolt back inside.

"Why? So you can freak out and run for the hills?" Basie tilted his head back, meeting Kit's gaze. "I don't think you're crazy. I promise. Now, will you sit?"

Kit thought about turning around and leaving Basie out in the nighttime chill, just to spite him. But he was too tired for childish games and in a battle of stubbornness, Basie would win every time.

He sat on the steps, as far from Basie as he could. The air between them seemed to warm, as if Basie was still carrying around the heat from the fire on his clothes. Kit knew that was impossible, but it didn't stop him from noticing that the breeze didn't bite as hard as it did moments ago.

Carefully, Basie sat up straight and placed the box he'd brought with him onto his lap. Kit had questions, but did not interrupt as Basie lifted the lid and procured a black and white picture. He held it out to Kit, who took it, and—

Great day in the morning.

He didn't let himself believe it at first, but the odds could not be argued with.

The picture was of a tan-skinned boy in a white, button-down shirt and knee-high shorts. His hair was cut short and slicked back, though some rebellious curls were sticking out in random directions. He was sitting on the Wellhead porch steps, clutching a brown paper bag, and splitting his face in half with a grin.

"That was my first day of kindergarten," Basie explained. "I don't remember a lot of things from those years, but somehow, I remember the lunch my ma made. I think I remember it because the other kids were jealous. All they had were peanut butter sandwiches and mushy apples. Meanwhile, I had a bologna sandwich made with fresh baked bread."

Kit felt like he was hearing things. Maybe he had fallen asleep against the window seat and his brain was showing him the wonderful things it thought he wanted to see. But then, Basie pulled out another picture, and Kit had to admit that dreams never sat so tangibly in his hands. According to Basie, this one was of him and his abuela in their best clothes outside her church. The date scribbled in the bottom revealed the picture had been taken in 1965.

One after another, Kit's lap filled with pictures, irrefutable proof that the one thing he would not allow himself to wish for had actually been true all along. It was all he could do to stare at them, tears gathering at the ends of his lashes.

"Well… Say something," Basie said nervously.

Kit wet his lips, but the inside of his mouth felt dry.

"This—" He cleared his throat. "This is *incredible*."

Basie sagged in relief.

"I'm glad you think so, because forever would've been a long time for you to hate me. Especially when you live just a quarter mile up the road." He collected the pictures, placing them back in his box. "Sorry it took so long for me to come back. I needed a few minutes to wrap my head around it myself. You're the first immortal person I've ever met, other than my mom. It's...it's a lot."

"I'll say," said Kit, voice small and reverent. Now that he wasn't holding Basie's pictures, his hands felt strange, like being so far from Basie's touch made them ache with the emptiness.

"And sorry for acting like you were fucking crazy. I just couldn't believe it. But you said it so– *easily. I* felt crazy for not noticing it earlier."

Kit chuckled.

"You *did* react like an aging person. They usually live in denial and say I must have an *excellent skincare routine.* But you shouldn't blame yourself. I keep a tight lid on it. Sometimes I just lose the details, like I did with the letter I sent your mom." He rubbed at his eyes, smearing away the wetness. "Does anyone else in town know? About you?"

"Lewie and the kids. Probably the folks who have spent their whole lives here. I've looked this way since the sixties. But they mind their business."

Kit must've looked nervous because Basie grabbed his hand and gave it a squeeze.

"They mind their business, Kit. Everyone has secrets and you being immortal is not even the strangest one I've heard since living here. You've got nothing to worry about."

"Alright," said Kit. "I trust you."

"Good."

They sat and listened to an easy quiet settle over the valley. Basie shifted so his back was leaning against the pillar of the porch, but his hand never left Kit's. When he met Kit's gaze, it reminded Kit of that time he'd asked Basie if he was prone to falling in love. *Not terribly, no,* Basie had said. Kit hadn't believed it then and he didn't believe it now. Not with Basie's attention turned on him like *that.*

"Will you let me take you to dinner?" said Basie. He spoke the words like they were honey in his mouth, slow and sweet.

Kit's fingers loosened in Basie's, but he didn't have the heart to let go.

"I won't let you take me out just because I'm the only gay immortal you know now," he warned gently.

The sweetness of Basie's words spread to his face in the form of a lopsided smile.

"I hate to break it to you, but I've been wanting to ask you out since you showed up at my door and told me you were named after your crotchety grandfather."

Red heat exploded over Kit's face. He hoped the dim nighttime veiled it away, but he'd never been good at hiding what he was thinking. If Basie's delight was any indication, he'd failed once again.

"You really liked me then?" Kit wondered, shyly.

Basie nodded. "Me asking you out was supposed to be the big reveal at the bonfire. I was gonna send my mom into the kitchen for more drinks. Then, I was gonna tell you that I've enjoyed getting to know you and that I'd like to take you out, so I can get to know you *more*. But Della Yeats is nothing if not a big orchestrator. She wanted the truth out in the open before I asked, because she thought you'd say no otherwise."

Kit's chest squeezed. He was sure Basie could feel his pulse racing under his skin.

"I might've," Kit admitted. "Only because I've loved mortal people before and it hasn't gone well. But, knowing what I do now…"

Basie inched forward, eyes bright enough to outshine the moon behind him.

"Is that a yes, Baltimore?"

There was a distinct danger in looking too long at Basie Yeats when he was beaming so beautifully. It felt like the affection that had been quietly brewing in the pits of his chest was now bubbling over, spilling molten desire over his insides and making it impossible to want anything else. Laughter welled in the back of his throat, but he wanted to speak clearly. He *needed* Basie to hear his sincerity.

"Yes, Mr. Yeats. I think dinner would be nice."

It shouldn't have been possible for Basie's smile to get any wider, but it did. He began to laugh in delight, which finally drew the same love-sick laughter from Kit. It was a strange sound for the nighttime—laughter was for the day—but Kit didn't notice a difference. Being around Basie was kind of like standing in the sun, feeling its invisible heat on his arms.

They were still looking at each other when their mirth finally fizzled away, but the endearment of it was still there. Basie, on his part, was looking at Kit like he had something to say. It was a lovesick expression, one that made Kit's spine feel electric.

"What?" Kit said, embarrassed.

"I just…" Basie shrugged. "I just wish I could kiss you *before* the date and not after."

Kit's flush was back in full force.

"Wait, that came out wrong. I want to kiss you before *and* after. I'd kiss you any time you let me, honestly."

"I–You–" He laughed, hiding his face in his hands, but Basie pulled them away. He was so much closer than Kit remembered him being. "You don't seem like the traditional sort."

"No," Basie admitted. "But you do."

"I could be persuaded."

That was all it took. A few simple words. Two hands in his. The sound of truth on his tongue.

Basie kissed him. It was a gentle exchange. Calloused hands on the apples of his cheeks. Kit's own skin resting overtop. Though Basie smelled like woodsmoke, he tasted of something sweet and real. The kiss stretched on longer than Kit thought it would, yet not nearly long enough at all. Maybe Basie felt it too, because he let his hands slide up in Kit's hair and tugged him closer. Kit had to catch himself before he fell straight on top of him.

When the kiss slowed, they pulled apart. Kit found himself leaning over Basie, whose chest was heaving up into his.

"I don't want to go home yet," Basie admitted.

"Then don't." He kissed Basie's throat, then immediately shot back. "Er–I don't mean–"

"No worries, I'm picking up what you're putting down," Basie chuckled. "I wouldn't let you ravish me that easily, young man."

He hoisted himself up off the steps and grabbed the blanket from the porch swing. Before Kit could ask what he was doing, Basie draped the blanket over Kit, then sat back down and brought the free end of the blanket over himself.

Basie laid his head on Kit's shoulder, slipping a hand through his arm.

It was the first time in many decades that Kit felt like a young man—not at all like he had a century tucked in his pocket. Vaguely, he supposed this is what it would've been like if he'd fallen in love for the first time in his quiet hometown and not under the raining shellfire of a great war. There was a part of him that had always longed for quieter beginnings than the ones he had. Maybe now, he could finally have them.

Basie listened to Kit tell stories about all the neighbors who has passed through the house over the last few weeks. At first, Basie would give insight. Things like, *Emily Long is the director of the library. Ask her real nicely and she'll waive any overdue fines you've got. Just so long as you keep checkin' books out.* The words petered out, like water from a dry spigot, until Basie was only listening. Then, he was only sleeping. Kit kept murmuring to him, like Basie would wake up and go home if he stopped talking.

Some time later, Kit's own eyes drew heavy. He combed his fingers through Basie's hair. It was just as soft as he'd imagined all those nights kept up by his own longing.

There was no need to stay up anymore, though. He could finally *rest*.

"Basie," Kit murmured, pressing a kiss to Basie's forehead. The man didn't stir. Rather, he cuddled further into Kit's side and let out a contented sigh. "Baaasie," Kit tried again—louder, but with softer edges. Basie's eyes remained closed.

"Basie, it's late," Kit said, this time at full volume.

"Yeah," Basie grumbled. "So quit talkin' and let me sleep."

It was unclear whether or not Basie was actually awake or if it was just the sleep talking. Torn, Kit looked up the road. He could try to carry Basie all the way to his bed at Wellhead Cottage. He was sure Della left the door open for him. But Kit's muscles were so sore from all the work he'd been putting into the house, that he wasn't sure he would make it all the way to Wellhead. The last thing he wanted to do was drop Basie in the dirt. His couch was always an option, but it was so new, it hadn't been broken in enough to be slept on—firm and unbearably uncomfortable.

…He could make it up the stairs to his bedroom. Probably.

If he slept on top of the blankets, completely on the other side of the bed, that was acceptable.

Right?

Kit wasn't sure he ever lifted a sleeping man and carried him to bed before. (Embarrassingly, he was usually the one being lifted.) It was with great care that Kit maneuvered Basie into his arms, holding him under the legs. He let Basie's head fall against his chest, thinking that maybe he was stronger than he thought.

Without any bumps or bruises, Kit carried Basie to his new bedroom. Strangely, the unfamiliarity of the room had subsided with Basie's warmth on his chest.

He laid Basie on the bed, then took off his boots. Immediately, Basie huddled further into the mattress. When he was out of his campfire clothes, Kit changed into thin pajamas and laid beside Basie. The drop of the weight in the mattress was what finally made Basie stir.

He blinked, then smiled when he saw Kit watching him.

"Is it alright if I sleep beside you?" Kit whispered.

This time, Kit could see the wakefulness spark alight in Basie's eyes.

"Don't even think about going anywhere," Basie grumbled. "Mind if I take my shirt off?"

Kit scoffed tiredly. "Oh, what a hardship to see a beautiful man shirtless in my bed."

Basie poked Kit in the stomach, making him release a bout of ticklish laughter.

"You could take yours off too, smartass," he replied. The combination of the words themselves and the gravel in Basie's voice made Kit feel like his insides were on fire.

He pulled his shirt off by the collar and tossed it across the room, while Basie laid his phone on the bedside table and stripped down to his boxers. With a lingering yawn, Basie draped himself over Kit's chest and let all the tension in his body drain away. It was almost too warm in the early summer heat, but Kit wouldn't have traded anything for the feeling of Basie's chest on his.

Maybe it was because the night addled Kit's brain, or maybe it was because he couldn't be anything but sincere, but he took the man against him into his arms and whispered, "Goodnight, a mhuirnín."

Basie smiled, warm lips moving above Kit's heartbeat.

"Goodnight, darlin'."

★★★

MORNING SEEMED LIKE A whole new day, even though Kit had gone to sleep a few hours ago. There was a kink in the back of his neck from sitting half-way up the headboard, but he didn't mind. The tiny ache only meant that Basie had slept comfortably on his chest all night long.

On the bedside table, Basie's phone began to vibrate so furiously, it nearly buzzed over the edge. Kit snapped a hand out and caught it before it could hit the floor. He lifted the phone up, expecting that the vibrating was some type of alarm. But the screen was actually lit with an incoming call from a contact named, "*Mam's Kitchen Rotary.*"

The rotary phone in question was a tired thing painted a color that was a far cry from its original 60s hue (Kit remembered what it was supposed to look like. He had one in his London apartment). There was a chance that if Basie didn't answer this call now, the rotary might not be strong enough to endure a second.

Kit drew close to Basie's ear, allowing himself just a second to breathe in his lover's scent. Basie's familiar scent of earthy wildflowers was masked under the lingering traces of the campfire smoke. The only downside to holding Basie to his chest all night was the certainty that the scent wouldn't linger on his pillow. A true shame, indeed.

"Basie, your mom is calling," Kit murmured.

He might as well have called out someone's name over their grave.

Basie's slow breaths fell warm over Kit's chest.

Was there harm in letting the man rest? Kit's own phone was in his drawer. He could just as easily text Della himself.

He picked up his phone to do just that, when the screen lit up. Loath to leave the pleasant comfort of Basie's arms, Kit turned the volume down and held the device under his ear. A raspy *Hello* was sitting in the back of his throat, but Della had already seized the first word.

"You hungry, darlin'?"

Kit rubbed his eyes, confused.

"I'm sorry, ma'am. Am I…hungry?"

"The Simons will be here in fifteen minutes, and I thought you and my son might like to fix up your plates before the children scoop up all the sausage links."

Kit's head fell back on his pillow, his free hand tightening around Basie's waist.

Of course. It was Saturday. And the Yeatses did "*big breakfasts on Saturdays.*" Kit looked down at Basie, who was mostly tangled hair and cute ears from this angle. He wasn't sure how to answer in a way that didn't allude to Della that he was currently in bed with her son. But it was morning, and he was most earnest when the sun was fresh, so he said, "That's awfully kind of you to think of us."

"Kind? Sweetheart, it's tradition. The fact that Basie didn't come home last night suggests to me that he intends to make you part of that tradition. And so do I, for that matter."

It occurred to Kit, somewhat strangely, that the last time Della had spoken to Kit was last night, when she'd been gently prying his secret from his tight hands. He'd left in such a rush, he hadn't been able to ask his own questions. It felt like a lifetime ago.

"Della…" Kit began softly. He leaned his cheek into Basie's hair. "Are you…How old are *you?*"

She snorted. "Hell if I know. You stop keeping track around three hundred."

It shouldn't have surprised Kit. He'd met folks who were pushing five hundred. It made his own pathetic century feel insubstantial—like there really *was* forever stretched out before him. The reality made him feel more human somehow. Kit Elliot was just like everyone else. He aged (albeit slowly), he made mistakes, and, one day, his ancient body would give out and he would die.

"You're thinking real hard, there," Della noticed.

"I'm just thinking that…" Kit sighed. "Don't you think it's a little strange how we all end up where we're supposed to?" He didn't have to clarify to her that *we* meant immortals. "Aging people have death chasing their tails at every turn. They rush into happiness like they're gambling for their lives because they *have* to. But there's no rush for us. We could spend our entire lives following our every whim and yet, we settled right where we belonged." This time *we* meant *Kit Elliot* and *Adella Yeats*. "I can't wrap my mind around it. How did we *know*?"

"How could one simple envelope with my name and address on it change your life, you mean?"

"*Yes,*" Kit breathed. "I've been all over the world, looking for home in all the places people would give their life savings to see. If I'm supposed to be right here, on this tiny patch of Pennsylvania, then that envelope with your address on it is a miracle."

"I reckon it is," Della replied thoughtfully. "You deserve quiet years, Kit Elliot. I'm glad you get to spend them here with us."

And—*great day in the morning*—the simple phrase made Kit *bleed.* He didn't think his mother had ever spoken to him with such gentleness, such reverence for his very existence. It wasn't that Della had cut him open. It was just that she had laid her finger on an old wound that was half-festering, half-sealed over, and forced the cut open. If he felt this exposed and raw, it was only evidence that little by little, the wound would mend.

"Do you—" Kit cleared his throat, willing his voice to comply through the thickness there. "Do you think I would've found Long Lily if I hadn't written you that letter?"

"I think so," she replied, voice drawing quiet. "I think even if I hadn't answered, you would've plugged the address into your fancy cellphone, taken one look at Wellhead Cottage, and shown up at our door with your U-Haul full of books. Maybe Lewie Simon would've shown you around. Maybe you would've met Lynn yourself and bought the house without any intervention necessary. But I think you would've made your home here. And I *know* you would've found Basie."

Kit's arms around Basie's waist tightened. A small, irrational fear nagged in the back of his mind that if he didn't hold tightly enough, time would shift back, and he would have to wander around the world until he found Basie among billions of people all over again.

"Thanks for your letter all those years ago," Kit said finally. And he *meant* it. Down to the marrow of his bones, he meant it. *Thank you for planting the seed I needed. Thank you for restoring the hardwood floors of my new house and sharing your pie recipes. Thank you for bringing the beautiful man in my arms into this world. Thank you for making him good.*

"You're welcome, Kit," Della said honestly. Her own voice was edged with tears. She let out a whooshing sigh, like she was unloading three centuries' worth of burden. "Now, are you boys comin' to breakfast or not?"

"Basie is still asleep. I've been having trouble waking him up. He sleeps like he's in a coma."

"Oh, he's awake," Della said certainly. "Don't let him fool you."

"He—what?"

Kit glanced down at the man lying on his chest where Basie hadn't moved a muscle. Not even a hint of a stir.

"His boyfriends always used to tell me I raised a cuddler."

That did it.

A hand snatched out from the Basie-shaped pile on him and tore the phone from Kit's hands.

"They told you *what?*" Basie demanded, voice was still raspy from sleep. Della's voice through the receiver dipped to the buzzing of a bee for all Kit could understand her, but Basie flopped flat onto Kit's front and banged his forehead into Kit's soft belly. "Oh my god, *Ma,* we'll be there soon. No—no, don't you breathe a word to Lewie." He glanced up at Kit, a flush pouring up his throat. "I'd kindly thank you to make like a good mother and mind your damn business."

Red warmth burned Kit's cheeks, as he snagged the (unused) pillow from the other side of the bed and covered his face with it.

"I'm hanging up now." A pause in which Basie did not, in fact, hang up. "*Yes,* I already said we were coming…Oh, for the love of—Goodbye*!*"

When the line finally went dead, Basie threw the phone across the blankets. It bounced a few times, then plummeted over the edge with a *thud.* Basie waved a hand dismissively when Kit started after it. He finally rolled onto the cool spot of the bed and gave Kit back control of his movement. The pillow Kit had grabbed was clutched tightly to his stomach and he found he could not meet Basie's eyes.

"How much of that did you hear?" he asked. *That* being, of course, Kit's moment of morning vulnerability.

Basie had the good sense to look apologetic.

"All of it," he admitted. "But I'm glad I did. I didn't know you felt that way."

"I thought that it might overwhelm you. If I told you."

"Why? I'm too old for things like fate to worry me."

"But—"

"But nothing. I've already decided that Long Lily is where I want to settle and that I like you quite a bit. Besides, my mom and I have never done immortality right."

Kit rubbed mindlessly at his chapped knuckles.

"Alright," he decided. He glanced up, meeting Basie's searching gaze. "For the record, I like you quite a bit too."

Basie propped himself up just enough to press a kiss on Kit's mouth.

"Believe me, I got the memo. But I'll let you remind me all you want."

Kit couldn't help himself. He fell into the welcome embrace of Basie's arms and kissed him again. The tan skin under Kit's hand was still warm from spending the night wrapped up with tangled limbs. But when he ran the pad of his finger down the slight curve of Basie's waist, Basie shivered. The kiss was a messy thing—lips barely touching lips from how wide their smiles were.

Somewhere in the back of Kit's mind, he remembered they were missing breakfast. Yet, they did not want to draw away from each other and end this moment before it was already begun.

So they didn't.

There would be forever for more Saturday breakfasts. Forever to sit under the murmuring willow branches and watch the bees of the Wellhead garden work. Endless mornings to look up into the endless Long Lily sun and think, *My, what a great day it is.*

Thanks for reading!

I hope you've enjoyed *Patchwork*! If you liked this novella, the best way you can help out is by rating it and reviewing it on its Goodreads page.

You can also find me on Instagram or visit TessCarletta.com to sign up for my monthly newsletter and stay up-to-date on bookish news.

About the Author

Tess Carletta is a library worker by day, and an indie writer every other waking moment. She holds a particular love for sunsets, quiet country walks, and stories about folks who love each other. She lives in Pennsylvania with two roommates and a round cat aptly named, Ruby the Ham Princess.

www.ingramcontent.com/pod-product-compliance
Lightning Source LLC
Chambersburg PA
CBHW022129310726
48972CB00007B/2260